WITCHCRAFT

AND OTHER FATEFUL TALES

by John Margeryson Lord

Order this book online at www.trafford.com
or email orders@trafford.com

Most Trafford titles are also available at major online book retailers.

Printed in Victoria, BC, Canada.

ISBN: 978-1-4269-0090-7 (sc)
ISBN: 978-1-4251-8928-0 (e)

*Our mission is to efficiently provide the world's finest, most comprehensive
book publishing service, enabling every author to experience success.
To find out how to publish your book, your way, and have it
available worldwide, visit us online at www.trafford.com*

Trafford rev. 2/16/2010

 www.trafford.com

North America & international
toll-free: 1 888 232 4444 (USA & Canada)
phone: 250 383 6864 ♦ fax: 812 355 4082

DEDICATION

This small book is dedicated to my readers, who may be few in number, but without them my efforts will have been a complete waste of time.

However, readers or not, I have very much enjoyed the work. Iwould like to add that it has kept me out of mischief - but I can't. I would also like to take this opportunity to thank whoever or whatever it may be which is the source of my creativity. I owe you a great deal.

JML
28/1/2009

CONTENTS

WITCHCRAFT

*A*nd no, I do not believe in the supernatural powers of witches.

----- And Yet?

I have an aunt whom I get to see only occasionally, mostly at weddings and funerals, but for whom I have a real and deep affection.

Agnes claims to be a witch - a `white' witch of course; that is to say she only indulges in witchcraft for good purposes. She has some indecent and vitriolic things to say about `black' witches, and claims to be at war with one such mis-guided person.

She lives and has always done so in a small village on the edge of Cornwall - a county for witches if ever there was one.

Now my wife and I have an elegant bungalow overlooking a small sheltered harbour on the west coast of the Scottish Border country where I run a small but profitable postal business from home, and Sheila, my wife, teaches at the local primary school.

Although we are not blessed with children we are content, leading a quiet life the main excitement being a regular visit to the Grapes, where they have a good selection of real ales; and gently tease the occasional holiday visitors.

Down in the harbour nestling at its permanent anchorage is our small sailing dinghy, the `The Spanking Lassie', which we take out sailing or fishing whenever the weather, wind and tide allows. I hasten to add that the name was not chosen by me, it came with the boat.

It was fairly early in the year and we had not had the boat out for some time when my lack of belief in Aunt Agnes's powers was brought into question, and in a life and death situation.

We had not heard from the darling lady since Christmas, but suddenly there she was standing in our porch as large as life clutching a small case and dripping from the rain.

When at last she had dried out and settled in front of the fire with a warming glass of Glenmorangie she said simply, `I just had to come to warn you'.

She had made the trip having taken two trains, three busses, and our local taxi - a journey time of some fifteen hours and she was very, very tired. She would not say any more about her reason for suffering this horrendous struggle to get here, and we did not press her. `It can wait till tomorrow,' she said, and took a grateful sip of the whiskey.

Neither Sheila nor I could guess what she might possibly have come all this way to warn us about. In spite of much worried discussion we would have to contain our curiosity over-night. We did not sleep well as you may imagine.

The next day being Saturday we had no pressing work to do, so all three of us sat down to a leisurely breakfast.

There was however a tenseness about the atmosphere as we were obviously keen to find out just why this visit was just so important, but Aunt Agnes kept us guessing until we had finished eating and were supping mugs of steaming coffee.

`I had to come,' she said, and paused to collect her thoughts. Her handsome and much loved features were furrowed with concern - whatever it was, she thought it to be extremely serious.

`Please, we are dying to know what this is all about,' I pressed.

At this Aunt Agnes looked sad and said, `That is a most unfortunate choice of words.'

And I started to worry.

`It is a life and death issue otherwise I would not be here,' she said very seriously.

Again she paused to think - then it all came with a rush.

`I was gazing into the future when out of the mists a very clear thought surfaced, that you,' here she pointed at me, `will face mortal danger. It will be touch and go if you survive, and it will be quite soon.'

We just looked at her too stunned to react. Then before I could ask the obvious question she continued -

`I do not know what form this will take but the feeling is very strong - stronger than ever now that I am here - on the spot as it were.'

Still neither of us spoke. Aunt Agnes held the floor.

What I badly wanted to know was will I survive? But before I could ask she replied as if she had read my thoughts.

`I'm sorry but it's not given to me to know the outcome, - however, I can help,' she said.

`I will use all my skills to lean on the good side and with luck I may be able to change the odds in your favour, it is all I can do,' she added sombrely.

Then very seriously, `It should just make the difference.'

After which, in spite of our many urgent questions, she would not be drawn to say more.

The weather had cleared and we were tempted to take a walk along the beach under a warming sun reflecting brilliant flashes off the rolling wave tops raised by a steady on-shore breeze. It was a grand day finishing up in good company at the Grapes where Agnes was made a regular fuss of by the locals. To our relief, the atmosphere seemed to have lightened somewhat.

Back at the bungalow the issue was not mentioned and Aunt Agnes was in good form recounting her experiences from her recent trip to Amsterdam where due to her action in the red-light district she found herself confronting the police. They, it seems, were sympathetic to an elderly lady with a sharp tongue who spoke her mind.

We retired after our usual noggin.

Sunday the second of May - a date I shall never forget.

Rising early I apologised to the ladies explaining that I had agreed with old Tom to take him fishing if the weather suited - and it looked to be turning out to be fine. The wind had reversed now being off-shore .

At this Aunt Agnes looked frantic.

`For God's sake don't go,' she said.

`Look the weather is OK, we've done this many times before, we'll bring you back some nice mackerel for supper or breakfast.'

`Please don't go,' said Agnes again, this time clutching my arm.

`Why, what can you see will happen?' I asked.

`I don't know but I have this feeling.' she replied.

`I'm sorry,' I said, `but I promised old Tom. You see we'll be fine.'

So, with a show of confidence I no longer felt I got the tackle together, kissed them both goodbye and set out heading for the harbour.

Old Tom was waiting for me at the harbour with his wide grin as I knew he would be.

We soon had the dinghy hauled in and loaded with our tackle. The little outboard, topped up with fuel, started on the first pull and with me at the helm we were off.

Once passed the harbour mouth we headed south. We always did. To the north I had been told lay unspecified dangers.

Well clear of the coast we ran out our spinners and patrolled up and down the usual haunts of coastal mackerel and pollack where usually on a day such as this with the tide rising and nearly full, we would expect to have caught several good sized fish each. Today - nothing.

We fished for over an hour without success - not even the tell-tale tug on the lines.

Then turning about level with the harbour we saw, some distance to the north, the `boiling' water on the surface that marked mackerel attacking a shoal of small fry, sand-eels perhaps. Then as often is the case the gulls arrived adding their noisome cries to the scene.

We discussed the possibility of boating over there to join in, and remarking that the morning ferry will have left long ago and would therefore not present a hazard, we agreed to give it a go.

The off-shore wind was more in evidence to the north, but in spite of the choppy sea we were soon at the spot. And it was worth it. We fished well and soon there were a dozen good sized fish in the bottom of the boat.

It was then that the first inkling of disaster appeared.

What we had forgotten was that it was holiday time and there was routinely a second, super-fast ferry, due just about now. Disconcertingly the throb of its giant diesel engines could just then be heard and was getting louder. Then there it was as it cleared the intervening headland - heading straight for us.

`Bloody hell!' Exclaimed Tom. `Lets get out of here.'

I spun the craft round and opened the throttle to full and we made off with the bows in the air and a creaming wake behind.

Towering above us the ferry ploughed past leaving a good area of free water between us and we breathed a sigh of relief.

But our satisfaction was misplaced. The ferry's wake was huge and it was upon us like an express - we stood no chance. The wake hit, lifted our little boat high in the air and dropped it crashing down tipping us out in the process.

My first concern was for old Tom.

To my relief his head appeared close by, but he was in poor shape. I swam over to him and held him up.

`Don't struggle,' I shouted into his ear, `I'll try to get us to the dinghy.'

The boat was only a few yards away and was now upright so I swam with the two of us towards it. It should have been easy but it seemed not to be getting any closer.

I then realised with horror that the off-shore breeze was taking the boat away - and out to sea. This knowledge I decided to keep to myself and re-doubled my efforts. But it was of little use, and soon I was tiring. Tom was silent and I was concerned for him, when suddenly my strength ran out, and all I could do was to tread water, worried that I may have to choose to save myself by letting Tom go. I knew the tide was on the turn and this would help me reach the boat - but not with Tom. I reviewed the chances of a rescue but even if the incident had been seen, which was doubtful, the lifeboat was a good half an hour away and by then it would be too late.

I confess I started to weep, and the idea of simply letting go passed into my mind.

Our situation was hopeless - without the boat we were dead.

I don't know how long this numbness of thought lasted, but I knew that I had given up.

And I prepared for the worst.

I could still see the dinghy - it was not far away - and strangely it seemed not to have got any father since I had stopped swimming towards it.

Then - it seemed to be getting nearer.

I did not understand.

Soon it was almost with reach.

'Hang on!' I shouted in Tom's ear, 'we might make it yet.'

I put in one last desperate effort to reach the boat which had now drifted very close, and was still moving steadily towards the land.

Thankfully we reached it and after a further struggle I got us both aboard. I lay Tom down in the bottom out of the wind and covered him with all the clothing I could spare. He was very pale but still drawing breath.

Then a real fluke - I managed to start the engine, and as I turned the bows towards the harbour it dawned on me why we had been saved - it was of coarse the wind.

The bloody wind - it was now blowing ON-SHORE and was taking us home.

* * *

There were people on the quay and someone sent for the ambulance which soon arrived and old Tom was whisked to hospital where with good care he soon recovered to regale the patient staff with increasingly lurid descriptions of the incident.

I was alternately labelled a fool or a hero, condemned by some and praised by others.

Back home Aunt Agnes made no secret of the fact that she had warned me, and made it plain that it was she who had changed the wind direction at the exact moment it was needed. And to my surprise my wife agreed, stating that Aunt Agnes had worried after I had left and had gone to her room where she was heard mumbling using a language that my wife had never heard before.

* * *

However things to do with Aunt Agnes and ourselves did not end there. The time came for her return, and we saw her into the local taxi with much good wishes and the odd joke from Bill Collet the driver.

Bill was a good but fast driver, and had chosen a route to the bus station via the country lanes. A tractor pulled out in front of the taxi and they had no chance of avoiding it. Tragically in the smash Bill was killed,

Aunt Agnes belted up in the back escaped unscathed. The tractor driver was treated for shock.

At the inquest the coroner was considerably puzzled by Aunt Agnes saying repeatedly the same phrase -

`I should have seen it. I really should have seen it.'

He had no idea what she meant - but we certainly did.

JML
24/2/2008

A NEAR THING

*M*urder. It was the last resort. He no longer could remember when this ultimate action crept almost un-noticed into his thoughts and stayed there insidiously refusing to go away. It was not that he took it as a serious proposition - he did not. It was just that it was there.

Before he saw Janice, Jan, for the very first time; an event emblazoned on his heart; he was a happy well adjusted lad enjoying university life with a keen interest in sport, drinking and all members of the opposite gender.

Regarded by the ladies as attractive he had a strong physique which he kept in good condition with a regular gym work-out. Tall and with a ready smile he had no trouble obtaining a partner at any of the frequent college raves.

Born and brought up by good solid parents who treasured their only child he had made the grade to one of our northern places of learning some considerable distance from his home town on the south coast, and his Mum and Dad missed him.

He was also a keen walker having discovered the rolling peat covered Pennines and the immensely attractive mountains of the Lakes District.

At home he was a hero, but here he was just one of the crowd an aspect of life he found hard to accept.

Andrew, Andy, Royston-Brown was also no slouch academically. He found his studies for a degree in law deeply fascinating and he developed an ambition to become a criminal lawyer. In this he would have done well but for the many physical distractions which came his way - instead his all too patient tutor thought that he would only just make the grade.

His first female conquest of many was a much older student who quickly realised Andrew's potential as a lover, made a bee-line for him and caught him with little trouble. In the few short weeks they were together she taught him most of what there is to know about the physical side of a man-woman relationship. They parted amicably enough when he discovered that she was actually engaged to a restaurant owner in the local town. To hers and everyone's surprise Andrew met and became a good friend of her fiancée, eating as often as finances would allow at the restaurant. He would be there most likely entertaining his latest target.

There then followed two or three casual and short lived affairs, after which Andrew found himself with a bit of a lean patch. He thought that his growing reputation was putting off would be conquests.

And then he met Janice.

In fact he didn't just 'meet' her he crashed into her. Literally.

During a training run one very fine April day in his second year he rounded the corner of the playing field changing room building at some speed and had no chance whatsoever of avoiding Janice on a keep fit jog going in the opposite direction. They both hit the ground in a messy tangle of arms and legs which took quite a time to sort out as both parties attempted to free themselves at the same time. Andrew was first on his feet, and reached down to assist the most bewilderingly gorgeous girl he had ever seen.

Long brown hair swept around perfect shoulders and framed a face that would be sharp featured but for soft lips almost always given to smiling. The lightest blue eyes flashed intelligently lending an air of commonsense to a look of bemused eagerness.

It was as if a devil may care personality was held just in check from breaking out at any moment.

As Andrew set Janice on her feet and apologised to her and asked her if she was hurt - he was lost. Lost - hopelessly and utterly. From the hair on his head to the soles of his feet he was lost. From now until he died - he was lost. From now on this stranger would govern his life.

Fate had decided and it was to cost him dearly.

Naturally they walked back to the halls of residence together, both trying to ignore recently acquired bruises. Andrew knew instinctively that if he tried any of his usual chat-up strategies he would loose her before he had begun, and for once he was hopelessly tongue tied, even nervous.

He decided to play it straight.

`I am desperately sorry for knocking you down like that - I'll take that corner wide in future.

`By the way my name is Andy, and I would like to do something to make amends,' he added hopefully.

But Janice's mind was elsewhere, and unusually for her she had taken an instant dislike to this very male person who looked at her with such open admiration.

`Thank you, but no it's not necessary, I'm sure I will recover,' she replied intending that this would end the conversation and the brief meeting.

`Please, won't you let me buy you a meal - I really do feel that I owe it to you?' Andrew persisted.

`Thank you again, but the answer is - no thanks.' His persistence was starting to annoy Janice who was hoping he would just go away.

Andrew tried again.

`At least tell me your name,' he insisted, now feeling cross at this obvious rejection.

Janice turned and started to jog away. Over her shoulder she called `Sorry, I have to run.'

Andrew stopped and watched her go, bewildered by this abrupt dismissal. He had a free afternoon and spent most of it alone puzzling over this meeting. Any other female and he would have shrugged it off probably classing the girl as a lesbian and think no more of it.

But in this case he could not get the image of her from his mind.

And so it was the same the next day.

And the next,

- and the next.

This then was serious, he found himself avoiding all other female company. He naturally resolved that the situation demanded action, and the first step was to find out who she was, not an easy task in a college with over a thousand a good portion of whom were female.

He rejected the idea of hanging around the ladies hall of residence - he would never live it down. Instead he listed all the girls he knew and set about asking each of them in turn. He would also continue to run that same route in case she chose it again.

For several weeks he drew a blank, then suddenly a stroke of luck.

He was assigned to judge a mock trial as part of his studies and there she was - a member of the jury, sitting there in front of him engrossed in the proceedings. But Andrew could not fail to notice that in the only glance she gave him there was no sign of recognition. He on the other hand could hardly keep his eyes off her. Dressed now neatly and becomingly in light pastel shades he thought she was even more deliciously seductive than before. He felt he wanted to protect her and seduce her at the same time. He determined to accost her at the end of the exercise and having made that decision tried hard to concentrate on the work.

At last it was over, and although he missed her, he did manage to catch a girl who was seated next to her and appeared to be an acquaintance. He learned her name and that she was studying legal history - the exercise had been a re-play of a famous early trial.

Now, he thought, how to break the ice?

Write? - No.

Knock on her door? - No.

Phone her? - Perhaps.

Then before he could do any of these he spotted her having a coffee in the refectory, and she was on her own.

His hand shaking enough to spill his own drink, he approached her with a turmoil of emotions - pent up desire, fear of another snub and of making a fool of himself, dread even.

'Hallo again, d'you mind if I join you?' Andrew began.

'Oh hallo! No I don't mind,' Janice replied in a neutral tone.

Not encouraging, he thought, but not an outright rejection.

`I noticed you in the jury - what did you make of it?' Andrew started on common ground.

Janice looked at him for some time before replying as if trying to decide what were Andrew's motives in starting this discussion. Then seemingly concluding it was safe Janice launched into a factual summery of how she saw the case. And to his surprise he learned that she had absorbed all the important aspects and had formed a clear and unique view of what had taken place.

He looked upon her with a new respect, she was clearly intelligent with a good clear logical mind and if he made any phoney move he would lose any hope of them becoming friends.

They discussed the case for a little while longer and then the topic changed to the college. It was all neutral stuff which did not get him any nearer to her, and he was due for the next lecture, so he struck out -

`I'm sorry, it's been most interesting but I have to go.' He paused, then -

`I would love to continue this discussion but in a more relaxing environment. Will you please let me take you for dinner, or lunch, or.............anything?' He added lamely.

And she floored him.

`I don't think my boy friend would approve, do you? We're practically engaged.'

This was something he had not considered. But it became instantly obvious that for such an attractive girl this was almost inevitable.

Damn and blast, he thought - now what? He was just not prepared to give her up.

Janice excused herself, and was gone.

Andrew sat there for some time gazing after her without a single thought in his head, but a pain was starting around his heart.

As luck would have it he saw quite a lot of her over the next few weeks, but without a single occasion to talk, and he saw the boy friend.

He was all prepared to dislike her feller but to his annoyance he found that the chap was much like himself even to liking the same out-of-school activities where he began to see quite a lot of him.

Ronald Slack was very much in love with Janice and it was abundantly plain when seen together that she was with him.

But he was not going to give her up, whatever it took he would make her his.

Andrew decided that Ronald would have to go.

He found himself constantly looking for her, and this she noticed and made a formal complaint to the college authorities. He was taken to task for stalking Janice and was told that should he give cause for a further complaint he would be asked to leave.

But Andrew was, as we have said - lost.

He could not, and would not give her up, it would be like losing apart of himself, he could no longer contemplate a life without her.

Ronald would have to go.

Andrew could no longer see beyond this simple fact.

His work and his health suffered as he became engrossed in plan after plan to prize Ronald away from HIS lovely Jan. None of these strategies was any good, they all had Janice blaming him for her loss.

What happened in the end was beyond any plan.

It was late spring and a good spell of exceptionally fine weather was encouraging walkers to make the most of it.

A notice appeared on the college information board.

"A GRAND WALK" - it announced.

"Will anyone interested in a day out by coach with a climb to the top of Helvellyn in the Lake District and a celebration meal and drinks afterwards in a local pub please add their names below. We can accommodate up to 25 persons. Please note - only those properly equipped will be allowed on the mountain which involves a climb of over 3000 ft. The climb will not take place if the weather is unfavourable, a boat trip on Lake Windermere will be substituted."

There then followed a list of instructions, assembly place and times.

When he saw Janice and Ronald's names on the list Andrew added his without a single thought or the slightest hesitation.

Fate had made its decision, and only bad weather could change it.

As it happened however the weather on the day was perfect.

Andrew was late and only just made it, and took his seat near the rear where he could just make out Janice and Ronald a couple of seats from the front; and then they were on their way.

The drive was uneventful, and the coach pulled off and stopped at Wythburn on the western side of Helvellyn.

Lakeland was at its best, the lower slopes and the intake fields were a brilliant green plashed white here and there with patient sheep. The sun already quite warm was burning off the thin wraiths of mist that were still drifting around the highest tops. It was truly a walker's day - what could possibly go wrong?

Much pleasant leg-pulling took place as walking gear was donned and adjusted and rucksacks slung.

'Don't worry Bill we'll collect you on the way back - you'll make it to the pub whatever happens.'

'I'll be on my second time round by the time you arrive.'

'Sorry Joe, we forgot your wheel chair.'

And they were soon away up the wide 'tourist' track in a straggly line, all proper with the leader at the head and the back marker bringing up the rear ready to assist anyone in trouble. Andrew found that he was enjoying himself so much that he almost forgot the lovers and effectively lost sight of them. They were still only a short distance up when the plaintive sound of a hunting horn wafted to them on the slight breeze. To this was soon added the braying voices of a pack of hounds.

The leader halted the group, gathered them round and explained that in the Lake District fox hunting was done on foot not on horse back and if they were lucky enough to see them to let them through.

They heard the horn several times and caught an occasional glimpse of the brown and white dashing shapes of some of the hounds but they were some distance away. Of the fox nothing was to be seen.

But the hunt was a talking point and friendly argument was inevitable. Andrew found himself with Janice and Ronald on the side of the hunters against almost all the rest who supported the fox and hoped that it escaped.

The mist just cleared as they reached the summit and making use of the man-made stone wind-break, opened lunch boxes and poured welcome cups of tea or coffee from flasks.

Unknown to them, they were minutes away from tragedy - which should be impossible on such a perfect day.

Andrew had wandered to the eastern edge of this famous mountain to take in the immense views of High Street and the glorious blue of Ullswater snaking away in the distance. To add to the atmosphere the sounds of the hunt could still be heard but now some mile or so away. He was almost happy.

Turning at the sound of footfall on the rocks he was surprised to see Ronald on his way to join him and take some photographs of the magnificent scenery.

Andrews mind was suddenly in turmoil as Ronald greeted him with a friendly wave.

`Blimey that's a cracking sight and just look at that drop - it's vertically down right at our feet. I'm glad it's not blowing a gale.'

`Yes,' said Andrew.

Ronald crunched clumsily on the loose surface looking for the best shots.

Suddenly there he was with his back to Andrew and between him and the precipitous edge.

His mind now a blank Andrew raised his hand to a point just level with Ronald's shoulder as the lad had the camera to his eye and was intent on looking at the scene through its viewfinder.

A push was all that was needed, Andrew looked around and the only people in sight were some distance away - they wouldn't see anything untoward.

It was a ready-made chance and he would take it.

-------- NOW.

But have we forgotten about fate?

A fully grown male fox, his rust brown coat contrasting with the pure white of his tail end, fleeing from the hounds and having made its way to the fell top suddenly, and unexpectedly lolluped up and over the stony edge. Startlingly confronted by the two men the fox gave a couple of barks, more of a yelp as a fox does.

Andrew jumped, turned to see where the unfamiliar sound was coming from, put his right foot and his weight on a loose stone which rolled away over the abyss - and Andrew now unbalanced was gone.

Ronald, absorbed by his photography heard but did not see the fox, but shockingly this was immediately followed by a sickening rattle of loose stones, and now neither could he see Andrew who, a second ago, was standing just there and now was not.

He realised that there was only one way in which Andrew could have so quickly and completely vanished was over the edge.

He found a spot where he could safely look down and peered over. What he saw he will never forget - there was Andrew lying broken on the rock strewn scree some two hundred or so feet below.

***

The leader chose Ronald and two others to wait with himself for the rescue helicopter which soon arrived, and with a certain clinical efficiency hoisted the body and took it away. The rest were requested to return to the coach. It was a very sombre group that eventually returned to college.

***

At the inquest the whole scene was played out on a large screen from a cam-corder recording taken from the summit by one of the party using its superb long range facility. Even the fox made its appearance.

But the one thing that was not seen was Andrew preparing to push Ronald over the edge - this action was hidden by Andrew's broad frame.

A verdict of mis-adventure was recorded.

As for the lovers - sadly the tragedy infected their relationship and Janice eventually re-met and married a rather sober family friend she had know from childhood and Ronald emigrated to Australia and married a chubby and very noisy local lass. They were both happy.

But it was a near thing.

JML
21/2/2008

THE NECKLACE

The jeweller threaded the precious stones each clasped in its own uniquely sculptured gold link very carefully one by one onto the simple cord, each to its allotted place, and there they lay on his bench loosely sparkling in the strong light, items of the jeweller's craft held together by the mother string. A loose construction with as yet no identity, an un-named thing. This was the time for which he had spent most of his life developing the necessary artistry and skill. Then, after a pause to savour the moment and holding his breath, he took the two free ends of the loop in his trembling hands, and raised the whole thing clear of the bench - and there it was - no longer a mere work object, no longer a simple collection of carefully selected but as yet unrelated meticulously crafted pieces, no longer a mere tangle of items each of small individual value, but on which much effort had been spent. Now it was that he gazed with justifiable pride at this object of rare beauty, which had mysteriously, even magically suddenly appeared. He knew this thing on which his critical eye now gazed was worth a great deal, much more in fact than the simple sum of the separate bits - and that, he knew, was his contribution.

As a craftsman he looked at this new piece of his workmanship with a mixture of awe and astonishment. And he allowed himself a gentle smile of appreciation as he beheld a creation of brilliant splendour - a unique and gorgeous piece that would one day grace a beautiful woman's slender neck. With years of hard won experience he knew that he had created a piece of unique and exquisite jewellery.

The thing he held was a necklace.

And it was a necklace born to give both pleasure and anguish.

The devil himself could never have created a more troublesome adornment - but this was in the future and thus unimagined by its creator.

He was not committed to any faith or creed, but he knew that God was the architect of this universe and all that was present in it. Deep inside himself he felt that he had been given a Devine helping hand, otherwise how could he, simple and untutored, produce something quite so perfect. It seemed to him that this was self evident and his lips moved in a silent prayer of thanks for his gift.

He savoured this moment, lingering over the almost overwhelming thrill that held him. His joy was however tinged with just a little sadness - his part was now over, the necklace would be passed on to someone new, and the more lasting pleasure would surely be that of that lucky individual.

Sad too he was that age was beginning to make itself felt, and he knew that this could well be the last work of such exceptional quality of which he was capable.

As he finally laid the necklace in its special case he thought, not for the first time, that wherever the necklace would be on display, and admired, there was an intangible something of himself being appreciated. It pleased him greatly.

Having thus satisfied himself that the finished work of art was as good as he could possibly make it, he put it to one side, reached into the bench drawer and extracted an identical case which he set by the side with the other, and gently opened its lid to expose the contents which lay there sparkling vividly in the strong light.

Even a skilled observer could be forgiven for mistaking this for a second necklace identical to, and of equal value to the first. But whilst they certainly looked alike they were inherently very different. This other piece was made up of inferior gems some of which were artificial, but at least they were set in similar quality gold. It was in fact the jeweller's test piece made up and completed to show what the final item would look like. The stones were cut in an identical manner as he had used these as practice pieces so as not to make a costly mistake with the genuine ones. He would normally break up such an item on completion of the real thing, but in this case it was so good he decided that, if displayed on its own it would probably sell for a respectable sum. It was in fact so good that it would take an extremely experienced and knowledgeable person to tell which was the one with the real value and which the replica test piece.

Our journeyman then discretely marked each box so that he at least would not make the mistake of selecting the wrong one.

The existence of these two identical looking pieces of jewellery eventually became quite famous and they were destined to cause grave international trouble bringing nations to the verge of war.

**

The effort that the elderly jeweller had put into this latest creation told on his health.

It had in fact taken many years of hard work to collect the stones, each one chosen for its grace and quality and its contribution to the whole. And he had told not another living soul in all that time.

That winter he contracted pneumonia and after a period of prolonged illness during which he was assiduously nursed by his deeply caring wife May Elizabeth, he succumbed and passed away just as people were preparing for Christmas.

May Elizabeth however knew very little of the jeweller's work or of the business. Happy that they were financially secure she contented herself with being mother to their two children and creating a warm and pleasant environment for them all.

Children, I use the word loosely, since Harold was a young and somewhat gullible twenty-five years of age, and his elder brother Nathaniel was a serious and studious thirty. The former had left university with a good degree and made a small living as a designer of business premises, the latter was also university schooled and received a sizeable income as a city financier - both men were happily married, but were thus far childless and lived close by.

Shortly after the jeweller had been laid to rest by the local church his wife and sons faced up to the painful task of sorting out his workshop. In this they had agreed that all three should be present, and it was as they were involved in this task that the pair of necklaces came to light. Nathaniel it was who opened the drawer and extracted the two identical cases and laid them on the newly cleared bench, moved the angle poise lamp nearer and opened both boxes. His shocked exclamation instantly brought the others over to look at what he had found.

All three gazed in wonderment at the sight that met their eyes. The sheer beauty and perfection of what they took to be an identical pair of jewelled, gold set pieces of sheer craftsmanship and skill stunned them. No-one spoke for some little time, and when they did it was with a quiet reverence as if they were in the presence of some deity.

It was clear to each that they had stumbled on something most unusual and inherently important, and probably extremely valuable.

Nathaniel it was who spoke first.

`By all that's in heaven,' he said, `I don't believe I have ever seen anything quite so lovely - and there are two of them.' Then practically after a pause, `Undoubtedly they will fetch us a small fortune.' He frowned, `I wonder when father made them and for whom they were intended.'

Young Harold looked upset at his brother's mercenary view of what were clearly works of art directly attributable to their father.

`Shouldn't we keep them in memory of him,' he said reverently.

`Good God no,' replied the practical Nathaniel, `what the devil would we want with them? You and I would have no use for them and on what glorious occasion do you think mother could wear them - they are much too grand. Besides just consider the money. In any case I believe he made them to be worn by someone perhaps famous and thus enjoyed and admired. We should honour this intention and get them sold.'

Harold tried again. `Perhaps he did intended at least one of them for mother.'

At this they both turned to May who had so far said nothing. She was gazing at the gems with a mixture of sadness and pain, her face pale with anguish. Obviously close to tears she did not reply immediately.

Then it slowly dawned on both men that as their mother was the legal inheritor of her husband's estate she it was who would decide what should be done with their new discovery, it had to be her and her alone.

Nathaniel quietly pointed this out and they both looked expectantly at May.

May was still trying to come to terms with her husbands early death and was finding it increasingly difficult to concentrate. She knew that she had to have time in which to try and understand what or for whom her husband had made these splendid pieces.

Just what had he intended? She had a natural wish to honour his plans.

`I do not know,' she began, `it's all so new and strange, I shall need time to decide.'

But she found it hard to accept that the necklaces really might be worth a great deal.

After some little thought , she said wisely, `it is quite clear to me that we will need to get them valued before any decision is made - they could be imitation and worth very little. I know who to ask and I will see to it. Until then we will do nothing with them.'

Having declared this she put them back in the drawer and gently pushed it shut.

It was only Harold who wondered why there were two identical pieces, but in spite of giving much thought to the problem came to no satisfactory solution. Like the other two he simply took them to be identical.

***

Now May Elizabeth knew just a few of her late husband's trade contacts and decided to invite the three with the best reputations to value all her husbands handiwork, inviting them at the same time to make her an offer for the each of the two necklaces.

And so in due course three meetings were arranged between the family and three jewellers each of whom specialised in slightly different aspects of the trade.

The first meeting was with Joshua B. head of Bank and Co - Advisers to The Crown.

After a lengthy examination of both items, he sat back looking most serious and professional, and said, 'Well now, I must confess I have never seen the like. They are both truly beautiful.' He paused and they held their breath.

'However, just one of these is right, and is extremely valuable, probably worth about two million Stalls. The other one is simply a practice piece and although almost indistinguishable from the other is worth only a fraction.'

And in this he had it correct.

'I recommend that you put the real one up for auction, my firm would be only to pleased to handle this for you - what you do with the other is up to you. perhaps you could keep it in memory of a good husband and father.'

With this he took the interview to be at an end, stood, bowed to May, and said, 'I shall look forward to hearing from you, when you have decided.'

'I don't trust him,' said Nathaniel when he had gone, 'he barely looked at the one he said was practically worthless. I want to hear what the other two have to say.'

Not a good judge of character, Nathaniel.

And so the second evaluation was arranged.

This time the examiner, a certain Sir L, was an expert in gold and knew little of precious stones, and since, as we have seen the gold settings were identical he declared with total confidence that both items were in fact identical - but worth very little. In stating this he had a plan to purchase both for a song and sell them secretly to known collectors for a nice large profit for himself.

`Believe me, you will be doing yourselves a favour to let me get rid of them for you, the market is rock bottom for jewellery at the present.'

But they knew him to be lying and quickly showed him to the door.

The third meeting proved to be more of a problem.

This time the man was an old friend of the family. He had visited many times and they knew him well and trusted him, but what they did not know was that whilst he had been a close companion of the jeweller he knew little of the trade. What little learning he had he had picked up from him during their long friendship.

So, there they were again sitting round the table on which lay the two boxes. The necklaces sparkled in the evening sun slanting in through the open window.

Mr Carl Z gazed in awe at the items under his inspection, and gingerly lifted each one in turn out of its box. Holding them carefully he turned them this way and that, first one and then the other. Very soon it was unclear which one was which and which had come from which box. Thus the careful work of Mr Joshua B was completely undone.

Turning the boxes over he noticed that one was marked and from his knowledge of how his friend worked he guessed correctly that one piece was a test piece, the other being the real thing. He then returned the necklaces to the wrong boxes without anyone realizing his mistake.

`I have no doubt at all,' he said with great confidence, `one of these is real and worth a small fortune, the other is not. This is the genuine one.' He said with an air of great confidence and patted the marked box.

But it was not.

They thanked him and saw him out.

***

After much soul searching May Elizabeth decided to sell both the `real' and the `copy' necklaces. The fact of their value and consequent risk of theft eventually crystallized her thoughts, and once decided she arranged for the country's most notable auction house Maximus & Co. to handle the sale.

This was the most valuable single item Maximus & Co had ever handled, and they were determined to write the occasion down in history. To this end the sale of the necklace for the estimated sum of 3 million Stalls was advertised internationally, and the date was set.

As provenance the auctioneers obtained from Joshua B a letter confirming that the necklace held in the box which he had marked was the genuine article. He was of course unaware of the swap.

The prospective sale attracted international interest, and the government of Silenia sent a small team of `experts' to look at the item with a view to presenting it to their royal family with the intention that it should be worn by their queen at her forthcoming coronation. The displaying of such a treasure would, they thought, bring them world-wide acclaim. The visit was a success and the money was voted to be spent.

Guards were posted everywhere, and the attenders were carefully security vetted on the big day. The sale was held not in the simple firm's auction room but in the magnificent royal library with its plush carpet, superb Flemish architecture, and world famous paintings.

As the auctioneers appeared on the platform a hush gradually fell on those present. Then as the security men brought in the necklace and mounted it on its prepared display stand a cry of wonder and appreciation filled the hall. It shone and sparkled beautifully in the strong spotlights arranged to show it at its very best. The auctioneers had ensured everything possible had been done to do justice to this now famous sale.

The audience held representatives of most of the world's richest nations.

Head of the auctioneers company mounted the rostrum and waited for quiet.

As the item needed no explanation or introduction bidding got underway immediately.

It drew gasps and applause at 2 million Stalls, and eventually was knocked down for a healthy 2 and three quarter million Stalls. It was a record.

***

Back in Silenia the necklace was handed over to the royal family with due ceremony.

They had, of course, no idea that it was not the real thing; in fact they had no knowledge as to the existence the other necklace.

***

The jeweller's family, now quite rich, wondered what to do with the remaining piece when they had a surprise call from Sir L who you may remember was the second of the original valuers and who would, he said, like to purchase the copy necklace secretly for his mistress. The sale was arranged and off he went, unaware that what he was carrying was worth a thousand times the amount he had paid for it.

Whilst every attempt was made to keep this transaction secret, nevertheless the underworld of criminals heard of it. And in the neighbouring state of Pinland Luis `The Lad', so far an un-convicted thief, was told of it and began to hatch a plan. He began to dream of owning the real necklace. His idea was simple to explain but he had no idea how to execute it. His plan was to steal the necklace held by Sir L's mistress and exchange it for the real one owned by the royal family of Silenia. Should he succeed he would without knowing it have presented the queen with the real thing.

He became determined, and decide on at least the first part, stealing from Sir L's lovely mistress should be easy, so he set about this eagerly.

As there was rarely any real news to report in the peaceful land of Silenia, the papers, in order to fill otherwise blank sheets, concentrated on the movements and prospective movements of the rich, the famous and the simply notorious. Thus our thief Luis only had to purchase the latest newspaper to discover where his target might be and when.

He discovered when Sir L's mistress would be entertaining representatives from Pinland at her home, and this was just what he was looking for. There would be safety in a crowd who could be relied on to be coming and going all evening.

For Luis the evening began badly as the necklace was being worn by herself, and he had to admire the effect. The lady was indeed handsome and our man almost forgot the purpose of his visit so impressed was he with the beauty of both necklace and wearer.

However his patience was eventually rewarded as the dancing got underway and the necklace was abandoned as the temperature in the hall rose to a discomforting level.

But it was never out of Louis's sight and he had it away minutes after it had been discarded casually in her ladyship's dressing table drawer.

It was some considerable time before Sir L's mistress had another occasion to wear the piece again, and by then trail had gone cold, the police drew a blank and Luis was safe.

The second half of the plan seemed to Luis to be impossible and he was still puzzling over it some months later. He was beginning to consider selling necklace, thinking it to be the fake, for what it would fetch, but then out of the blue the means came easily to hand.

As with all royal households that of Silenia was proud of its possessions and decided to put them, albeit heavily guarded, on display for the world's public to admire, and to caress their sensitive egos. Louis guessed correctly that the heaviest attendance to view the crown jewels would be in the first few days of the showing. Gathering some colleagues together he arranged for a diversion serious enough to distract the attention of the guards just long enough for him to execute the swap.

It worked like a dream, whilst the police and the military were arresting the chap who had fired several rounds into the air from an ancient rifle, Louis had made the exchange.

**

Thus - the Queen of Silenia now had the real thing, and Louis, now safely back in Pinland had the copy believing it to be real.

Louis now needed to change his necklace for money and started to talk about his claim of possessing the real necklace to certain underworld persons of influence and power. Word leaked out. Whispers abounded, and inevitably some came to the ears of certain ruthless members of the Pinland's popular press.

The Pinland newspapers were no different from those elsewhere in the world having their own kind of mathematics. For them two when added to another two usually made at least five and was sometimes rumoured to make an even six. They jumped on this story and having for some little time tried to gain a political edge over their neighbouring Silenia, went, as they say, to town.

Thus it was that the good citizens of Silenia awoke one fine spring morning to find their breakfast ruined by learning from their own press that headlines in Pinland read -

`Silenia's Royal Familly Display Fake Jewellery'

And -

`Where are Silenia's Genuine Royal Jewels?'

And worse -

`Pinland man holds the Genuine Crown Jewels of Silenia'

This slight was taken extremely seriously in both states. Diplomacy ceased in the climate of claim and counter claim.

The temperature of friction went up even higher when Pinland claimed that the real crown jewels were here in Pinland although they would not say where.

Pinland raised doubts as to the integrity of Silenia's Government, whilst Silenia charged Pinland with trying to create a war situation.

Diplomats were withdrawn from both sides. The UN advised visitors to leave both countries and cancel any future travel arrangements.

Silenia, `as a precaution,' they said moved a squad of tanks up to the border and mobilised two battalions of crack troops, its total military capacity. Pinland blockaded Silenia's only port with a battleship and two destroyers, its navy's total complement.

Inevitably other countries began to take sides and the situation became critical.

Both nations raised their alert status to pink in the case of Silenia, orange in Pinland, just one short of red, and warned their citizens to prepare for conflict.

Volunteers were called for and squads of ordinary folk armed with everything from pitch forks to blunderbusses were seen parading about the streets.

The air was thick with the smoke from flags being ceremoniously burnt.

Two of the earth's most powerful nations sent their highest level representatives to both would-be belligerents to mediate for a peaceful settlement.

Noise of War was in the air, and the world held its breath.

***

The jeweller's family came under pressure to settle the argument by confirming the Royal necklace as genuine.

May Elizabeth was frantic with worry and called her sons to a meeting.

`What on earth shall we do?' she asked tearfully when at last the three were sat together.

`That's easy,' retorted Nathaniel scornfully, `we must get Mr J to confirm the Royal necklace as genuine.'

`I agree,' said Harold, `he identified the right one in the first place.'

But May was not so sure.

`What if the other one turns up? After all we have no idea where it is, and that could be the genuine one.'

Nathaniel was practical. `As I see it we have no choice, if we do nothing a war will start, a war for which we will be held responsible.'

Reluctantly the other two agreed and Mr J was sent for.

But Mr J had more sense than to be placed in such a critical position and aware that this might happen he was out of the country and un-contactable.

May Elizabeth called a second family meeting.

'What in heaven's name do we do now?' She pleaded.

Her question was greeted by a shocking silence.

***

Sitting on the cause of all this mayhem Louis started to get extremely frantic. He lost all his intention of selling the necklace, and was genuinely concerned that it might be the cause of war and a serious loss of life. He was afraid that quite a few people now knew that he it was who possessed one of the contested items, especially as he believed it to be the genuine article. So after several days of sheer panic he decided to surrender the thing anonymously. But to whom?

After much cudgelling of his mind he opted for the simplest means he could think of.

He wiped the necklace and its box very carefully to remove all traces of his finger prints. Then wearing gloves he purchased a large envelope and addressed it to Pinland's chief of police and posted it via the farthest public letter box from his home that he could find. His sense of relief when he had accomplished this was so strong he was so euphoric that his friends thought that he was seriously drunk. It was all he could do and waited in fear for events to unfold. But nothing happened.

In due course the package arrived at the police HQ and was collected as usual by the chief's secretary. Now the chief had been receiving lately a series of packages of insulting and often disgusting material probably, it was thought, from some criminal he had been responsible for sending to prison. And so it was simply dumped with the others unopened. But after week or two the pile of such envelopes was getting in the way and the chief had them all opened and examined for evidence as to the sender.

Meantime the international situation was getting worse. Half the worlds nations had taken sides and armies long unused were set to intensive training. Military hardware was wheeled out, oiled and tested in view of the world's press.

When Louis's package was eventually opened and its contents discovered, its likeness to the Royal jewel was unmistakable. The chief was unable to give a satisfactory explanation for the delay and had to resign.

The newly appointed chief took matters in hand immediately, called a press conference, where, under armed guard, the necklace was displayed for all to see.

To his surprise, instead of solving the issue, things got considerably worse.

Everyone suddenly became an expert and every range of theory for the appearance of a second piece looking identical to that of Silenia's Royal family was expressed.

What was worst was that both nations claimed they had the real thing.

Experts were called in, examined the items but could not agree.

Impasse.

Then, just as violence was about to explode, the jeweller's family were interviewed and let slip that Joshua B of Bank & Co - Advisers to The Crown had examined the original pair of necklaces and knew which was which. He was contacted and reluctantly, to prevent all out war, agreed to look at both items and declare each either false or genuine. Such was his reputation and that of Bank & Co - Advisers to The Crown, that both parties agreed to abide by his judgement.

***

The day dawned cold and grey as Joshua B was escorted via a military vessel to an island situated in no-man's land half way between Silenia and Pinland. They took him to a large, bleak, and imposing castle. As he was then shown in, he heard the unmistakable sound of doors closing behind him and keys being turned in locks.

A table and one chair occupied the hall which was lined by armed soldiers of both nations. The table was illuminated by a strong light and a set of jewellers implements of inspection lay to the side of two boxes each labelled with the crest of the two adversaries. He was instructed to handle only one item at a time to avoid any further mix-up.

As Joshua B of Bank & Co - Advisers to The Crown sat and picked up the first necklace, the world held its breath.

Joshua B of Bank & Co - Advisers to The Crown took his time.

He was clearly under great stress as he carefully inspected the jewels.

The only sound in that vast hall was that of the gentle clicking of the stones as he carefully inspected each necklace in turn.

After what seemed to the watchers to be a lifetime, Joshua B of Bank & Co - Advisers to The Crown stood and announced they would have his report in twenty-four hours and that he would present it first to the Queen.

Joshua B of Bank & Co - Advisers to The Crown wanted time to think.

***

The time was up.

Joshua B of Bank & Co - Advisers to The Crown had till noon to deliver his findings.

He was just ready when a limousine flying the Royal Crest and in the centre of a small convoy, arrived to take him to Royal residence. After too short a journey he was assisted out of the car and with a security guard on either side our man was escorted to entrance of the Grand Palace. As he left the car he was assailed by the noise of the press of both countries numbers of whom were being held back by the police.

The whole world's attention was on this event.

By contrast the atmosphere inside was silent almost venerable.

Eventually he found himself in the Royal reception room and was left there on his own but for two palace guards one on each side of the entrance, to prevent his escape he assumed. Looking around he found himself surrounded by secure show cases displaying the Royal State jewellery collection for visitors to admire, including that of the item in question. He took full advantage of his enforced wait to study these pieces of finery and what he saw intrigued him greatly.

He had just completed this careful inspection, when her Royal Majesty was announced, and she entered escorted by a pair of household staff, - and her mother. Her demeanour on entering was serious and it was clear that she was trying to hide the fact that she was considerably nervous as to the outcome.

She did not smile as he was introduced to her and the Queen Mother

He bowed to both.

The Queen nodded nervously for him to begin.

He handed her his report.

She handed it to one of the staff who broke the seal, removed the document and on her signal began to read the contents out slowly and in a clear, educated voice.

The report was six detailed pages long and addressed every single stone on both necklaces.

It was thorough and impressive - it had to be to be believed.

- And it was.

It concluded that -

"Finding No.1 - Both necklaces were well crafted and hard to distinguish between.

Finding No.2 - One of the pair was a jewellers test piece of little worth.

Finding No.3 - The other one was a fully finished item and was therefore a `proper' or `right' piece.

Finding No 4 - Finally the item listed in 3. above was that which he understood to belong to the Royal Household of Silenia."

***

So that was that.

The press released the report to a waiting world. The armed forces were disbanded, and normal diplomatic relationships resumed. The world breathed a sigh of relief.

Or was it?

***

It was some months later that Joshua B now retired from Bank & Co - Advisers to The Crown paid a courtesy visit to the jeweller's family.

They were puzzled by this, dreading some terrible further revelation. May Elizabeth was for the umpteen time blaming her husband for getting them into this mess.

Joshua B was shown in as May Elizabeth, Nethaniel and Harold took their seats and sat expectantly.

A most stern looking Joshua B began with a dire warning.

`You must swear on your lives that what I am about to tell you - you will never divulge, I would have kept it to myself, but I have a need to tell somebody.'

The family were shocked, what on earth were they letting themselves in for? but after a stunned silence and a brief discussion they swore to keep his secret.

`My report did not lie,' he began, `but it did not tell the whole story. The actual facts are hardly believable.'

He looked round the table. He had their full attention.

May looked worried, Harold frightened clearly out of his depth.

Nathaniel defiant, ready to defend them to the bitter end. Impatient our Nathaniel.

Joshua decided to finish what he had started -

`To start with - one necklace - that is the one which the Royal family and the world now accept as the real thing, is of an exceptionally good quality, as in my report, but, in fact, it is the one which was made by your husband,' he nodded at May, `as the test piece.'

Nathaniel was the first to recover.

`By God no one had better find out or it will all begin again, but what about the other one?' He added. `Is that the real thing?'

`That is very strange, for whilst the other one they showed me is an excellent copy it was not made by the same hand being most inferior in many respects, worth very little; and I have no idea who created it or why.'

`Well then where is the real thing? And what happens if it should turn up?' Harold voiced what was in the minds of all three listeners.

`In that event, I have no doubt that they will call on me to identify it and I shall tell them that it's an exceptionally good copy, but one not made by the same person, a person not known to me.'

If that was not strange enough what he said next shocked the other three, leaving them speechless.

Joshua B waited as if to consider what to say next.

May was fearful of the consequences of the possible re-appearance of the real thing, whilst her sons were trying to think of a way out of the dilemma this would inevitably cause.

Joshua B began again. `I now believe that such an event will never happen,' he studied their faces, `you see, I took a good look at the rest of the Royal gems which were on display and there was a pair of earrings and a couple of dress clasps which were made of beautiful pendant jewels.

`Now the strange thing is - these items had clearly been removed from the original real `right' necklace which is where I last saw them - and I clearly recognised that which was to me the unmistakable handiwork and cutting technique of your husband,' he nodded at May.

`Of this I have no doubts whatsoever.

`- which is why it must remain our secret.'

He then sat back and looked at three shocked and puzzled faces.

***

The so called fake necklace was now so famously notorious that although genuinely worth very little, when it was eventually auctioned it went to a secret group and fetched enough to build two new hospitals one in each of Silenia and Pinland.

They were both named by the group The Royal Jewel National Hospital.

JML
15/8/2008

THE BEYOND

*I*t's not often in this modern world that someone experiences that which can be genuinely described as - unique. Almost everything has been done at least once before.

But in this case it was unique, and as far as is known it still is, although many attempts have been made since for it to be repeated - they have all failed.

It was some considerable time ago and the people involved have all now all passed on, so this description of these strange events has been assembled from snatches of conversations recorded at the time and notes written by those involved, that is what little written or recorded information has come to light.

As far as can be ascertained it all took place around 2008 some fifty years back.

At that time, science and technology were starting to make real breakthroughs in cures for common deadly ailments, and the frontiers of human knowledge were being pushed forward in both particle physics at one end of the scale and outer space at the other.

Surprisingly however, in spite of all this, and subsequent progress in these and related fields of science, it is only now that a convincing explanation for what took place has been promulgated, although there seems to be no limit to the numbers and variety of discarded theories. If anyone or any agency did know at the time they were keeping the information very much to themselves.

So then, what can we make of the available evidence? As far as I can gather, it all started when a very normal group of explorers laid plans to study an otherwise un-visited and extremely remote mountainous region in northern Chile. Five of them set out and five returned, but family and friends who knew them well reported that although those who returned bore every resemblance to those who set out, they were not quite the same. The changes were subtle but real.

I have chosen to write this from the point of view of Ron Stapleworth since his diary seems to be the most comprehensive. Ron was twenty-five at the time, had a degree in nuclear physics, and was a keen and very fit rugby player. He wanted to do something different before he took up his newly acquired job working on the LHC that is the Large Hadron Collider, a major International project. And a more feet-on-the-ground, less imaginative guy would be hard to find.

He begins -

There were five of us, Bill Wilde - our tame geographer, John Stamp a biologist - no field of expertise but definitely the real organiser of the team, we couldn't have managed without him, Sally Freeman - a doctor in medicine, and a good one, Beharn Woolington - she was a linguist and archaeologist hoping to find some ancient script, and of course me trying to contribute but in reality spending most of my time attempting to understand the others. All in all we were a mixed bunch but with a useful breadth of knowledge.

Also we were all reasonably fit having passed a basic health and fitness check before committing to the trip.

The group had got together in response to Bill's Internet advertisement and had met several times on a semi-social basis to prepare plans, agree responsibilities, and generally get to know each other. At the last of these preparatory sessions we were all looking forward to the trip and drank a toast to its success.

The journey out to the capital, Santiago, was only notable in that Bill made a play for the very attractive Sally; was turned down flat and got somewhat drunk. Fortunately Bill had a good sense of humour and as able to laugh it off in spite of being much teased about it, much to everyone's relief.

- Still, it did show by our reactions that we were all fairly normal well balanced people, which was important as we were to be in each other's company for several weeks with only minimal communication outside the group.

Yes - a word about communication, we were able to borrow, on a trial basis, rather neat items of hardware with which we could, more often than not communicate with our colleagues and friends back in England. In the event these gave us something of a false sense of security.

Once in the capital city we made contact with the university which had kindly financed the expedition in exchange for the data with which we were expected to return. They even provided transport in the shape of two fairly sturdy and well equipped four-by-fours.

We discussed and agreed our plans with our sponsors, and collected two week's worth of provisions for the first of what should have been several trips of exploration.

Our aim was to explore an area on the slopes of a nearly 6000 metre high mountain called Sillajhua, the nearest town with an airport and reasonable road links being Iquique. We were visiting the area on behalf of the university to look for some remote caves within which there had been reports of some unusual artefacts. The flight to Iquique was rough but we arrived more or less in reasonable fettle, collected our vehicles and loaded our provisions plus a variety of scientific instruments some of which were ours and some borrowed. As none of us were familiar with the area, the three men tossed a coin - the looser being the route finder and guide. This critical task fell to Bill which everyone else thought being the geographer, was in fact the best choice. He immediately immersed himself in what crude maps we had been given, - and succeeded in getting us lost even before we had left the town. I have to say however he performed magnificently thereafter otherwise we would not be here to tell what took place.

In the first few days we got acclimatised to the conditions, initially hot but getting ever cooler as we climbed over rough tracks, over rushing rivers, and through thick forests of huge trees. Many times we had to effect a de-tour. I think it took us about two days to reach the intended area of operation and find a good camping spot by the side of a fast bubbling stream of clear fresh mountain water. We dug in and it began to feel like home.

Bill, John and myself sat down and divided the area into six sub areas which one by one we planned to explore on each of the next six days with a rest day off in the middle.

Well - what was the atmosphere like in the group at this the start?

Broadly, it was one of anticipation. The attractive Sally had given up worrying about the condition of her skin, was trying to be nice, but not too nice to Bill who still looked longingly at her when he thought he was not being observed.

Beharn kept herself to herself, hated cooking and griped continuously when it was her turn. It was she who most needed contact with home and used the communication equipment every day. She was small and neat, nice looking but not a stunner like Sally.

Bill thought of himself as the strong man of the team and insisted in taking on all the tough jobs like chopping wood, and pitching our tents almost single handed.

John was a quiet man who prided himself in being able to fix just about anything that went wrong. He was full of common sense which was sometimes a bit of an irritation.

I was happy just doing what ever I was asked to do, and tried to keep an accurate diary of events.

Our surroundings were magical. The day was alive with the sound of bird calls and everywhere there was something new to look at. The nights were soft and gentle under the huge trees.

We were all conscious of the fact that we had to return with something usefull.

It remains debatable that we did.

**

Day one, and there we all were, all kitted up and eager to begin.

`Well now, here we go, this is what it's all about. I really am looking forward to finding the pot of gold - and to not sharing it with you,' quipped Bill.

`Then I suggest we concentrate on finding it before we decide what to do with it,' I remember suggesting, `let's get this bloody machine going and try and make some progress to the north.' With us all plus equipment in the one vehicle we were somewhat cramped. The other wagon was left at camp to save fuel and act as a spare. The track was rough and in spite of the driver's attempts at providing a smooth ride and we all found ourselves with a fine collection of bruises. Turns were taken at navigating and driving, and I have to admit that the best drivers were the girls whilst I was acknowledged as being the worst.

`Can't you just aim for level ground?' Beharn complained bitterly.

`I would,' I responded, `but there is none.'

`Even so, there is no need to pick the worst,' she replied. So we bounced along for several hours, after which we took an alternative route back to our base camp.

Round the fire, and having eaten, we fell to discussing our disappointing day. In spite of seeing many likely cliff faces, which should according to the geology be riddled with caves created by fast running water making its way from the vast upland slopes above us down through our forest to meet in the big rivers far below.

`Not a sign, all day,' Sally grumbled.

`Blimey! We've hardly begun,' declared John, `give it a bit of a chance lass.'

`Yes but from what the locals were saying I expected to see hundreds of likely caves,' she replied.

`Eye, but you can't rely on them, not a single one had been anywhere near here. We're breaking new ground.'

`Yes and most of it's in my boots,' Beharn said wrily.

***

The days of the first half of our exploration passed in a similar manner and likewise without result. Back at base camp, sitting round glumly, we began a full discussion of our position. It was very clear that our strategy so far had failed, and it was essential to change it for the secong half - but to what?

`I suggest we keep going in the same way, but father afield,' was John's suggestion, typically for him unimaginative.

`That's hopeless and depressing', said Beharn, `surely we must try something very different. We are running out of time.'

At this I had to agree.

Then Bill and Sally together chipped in, `Yes it's no good just doing the same old thing over and over again, It's boring,' grumbled Sally. `Agreed, I'm just about off my head with it.' put in Bill.

And so it was. A change of approach was needed, but to what?

Strangely we all sat round like muffins each waiting to hear from one of the others of a new and bright idea - a breakthrough even. Not one of us had a suggestion let alone a useful one.

John eventually broke the silence, `Why don't we sleep on it and discuss any proposals after breakfast tomorrow?'

To which we all agreed with some feeling of relief.

***

The next day dawned with the clear blue sky we had become accustomed to. And the only constructive proposal for a change came from Bill.

'Look,' he bagan, 'I have been studying the maps and adding our knowledge of what we have seen so far. It seems to me that not only may we be in the wrong area, but we should be somewhat higher up the cliffs than we have been so far. We also need to look more carefully. So this is what I suggest -

'One - we pack up both vehicles and leave this place in favour of camping where we land up at the end of each day.

'Two - having noted a likely place we leave the vehicles and explore on foot.

'Three - if the chosen area shows no promise we move on immediately.

'In this way we will cover much more ground, and being on foot will be in a better position to find just what we are looking for.'

At this he stopped and looked round at us all, his expression a question.

I think we were all relieved at the prospect of doing something radically different, so instead of agreeing we all fell to discussing how best to organise this new plan, and so it was adopted by default. First a day of rest was voted for and everyone used it well. The provisions and equipment was split intelligently between the two vehicles. And a novel idea of John's was adopted - this was that the occupants of each car would be rotated daily as driver and guide.

Having everyone take their turn at deciding our route meant that we shared equal responsibility for the success or failure of the search. We all, each one of us wished we had done this from the start.

***

It all happened in day three of the second half of the trip, and Beharn was the day's guide. During the night there had been a tremendous storm and much water was streaming down the cliff face. She had chosen a route high above the night's camp having spotted, she said, a narrow track above what she thought was what we were looking for. We set off on foot. A track it proved to be but progress was difficult at times as we had to negotiate fast and sometimes deep tumbling water as it forced its way across the track and down the cliff face. And then suddenly we came unstuck.

Struggling through one such waterfall, without warning the stones making up the track started to role away from beneath us, and we found ourselves falling in a mass of tumbling earth and rocks dislodged by the force of the water. Fortunately we did not fall far and came to rest on a broad ledge, banged about and horribly wet. As we were sorting ourselves out amidst loud complaints aimed at Beharn's regrettable choice of route, there was an excited shout from Sally and all injuries were suddenly forgotten.

`Look,' she shouted, `right there.'

We all looked to where she was pointing and there at the back of the ledge was what looked suspiciously like the dark entrance to a cave in the cliff face. There was then an undignified scramble over loose rocks and then at last we stood silent and awe struck   gazing at a vertical fizzure in the rock face which showed the marks of human endeavours to enlarge it. It was clearly the entrance to a cave of some kind.

Sally was the first to find her tongue. `We seem to have found something interesting, let's hope there is something here worth reporting. So what do we do next?'

Bill assumed control.

`Firstly let us have a quick look to check that it is worth exploring, and if it is we must return to the trucks to get changed into caving gear and collect lights, instruments and recording equipment. I think there will be enough of the day left after a quick snack to do some serious work here.' So we scrambled the short distance back and were soon eagerly busy with preparations.

It seemed like no time at all before five well equipped and very excited individuals stood again outside the dark entrance to what we hoped would produce some unique or at least interesting finds.

We had no idea just how unique this was to prove.

As the finder, Sally was elected to lead the way. Almost immediately we found ourselves in what was clearly a man made tunnel with a level floor carved out of a natural fissure and enlarged to permit the passage of an average sized human. It soon bent first left and then right and daylight from the entrance no longer reached us.

Afterwards opinion differed as to how far in we went before we reached the point where the tunnel opened out into `the chamber'.

We crowded in, and for the second time that day stood silently in amazement. Around us was something much stranger than we had ever imagined we might see. The `chamber' was by any standard huge. It was almost precisely rectangular in layout being about 80 feet wide by about 100 feet long, and a staggering 50 feet in height.

We looked around in wonderment, I remember thinking what in heaven's name had we stumbled upon. This place was man-made, and it suddenly struck me it was for some definite purpose. But what?

Beharn suggested before we wander all over the place we stop where we are and make a record of what we can see. The big pressure lights were lit, the camcorder , and the still camera were brought into action and Behan started to speak quietly into her miniature recorder.

I made a sketch of the layout which is shown on the next page, but some explanation is required.

The floor was level and reasonably smooth but was divided centrally along the chamber's length by a narrow, about one inch wide, crack. This crack continued up each of the end walls and even across the ceiling. It had the effect if dividing the chamber into two more or less equal halves. Each half was a reversed mirror image of the other, and as we had entered at one corner of the chamber there appeared to be a second tunnel at the farthest corner. Six large stones acted like seats, three on each side.

But what was the most fascinationg aspect to the whole thing were the floor markings. In the first place they were made out of some kind of yellow metal, I guessed brass, which was let neatly into the rock of the floor. There were two large arrows, and on each side of the crack was some script. Each of the arrows pointed to the other half of the chamber. Beharn said she had no idea what the script was or what it meant.

One further, and very strange thing about the arrows was that someone had taken one of the small red stones that littered the floor and used it to scratch a cross on both arrows as if to cancel them.

Or as a warning?

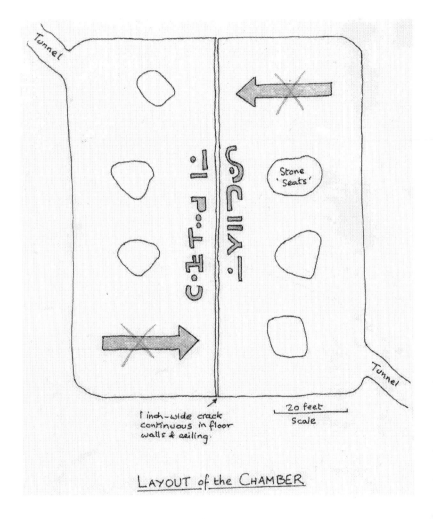

Tunnel

Stone
'Seats'

Tunnel

1 inch-wide crack
continuous in floor
walls & ceiling.

20 feet
Scale

LAYOUT of the CHAMBER

We spent about an hour making notes and recording all we saw, after which Sally, Beharn and John sat down on the stone 'seats', Bill stood with me by the side wall. All of us had stayed in the first half of the chamber, that is on our entrance side of the crack.

The crack intrigued me, and I strode over to it, still keeping strictly to 'our' side, and peered down it. I found that it seemed to go down for ever, no bottom was visible.

On an impulse I took out a small coin and dropped it into the crack. It was an old schoolboy's trick to gauge the depth. What happened next took us all by surprise and left us wondering just what this place really was.

The coin left my hand and was soon out of sight in the dark depths of the crack and I started to count the seconds for it to reach the botton with the usual clatter. I had reached ten with as yet no returning sound when there was a zizzing noise and the whole crack from the floor, the walls, and the ceiling was lit for about a second with a vivid bright green light.

Startled, I jumped back out of the way, and waited for my sight to recover, but nothing else happened.

'What the hell was that?' Shouted Bill, 'what the dickens did you do? For heaven's sake don't do anything else.'

'We seem to have discovered something very different from what we expected and came here to find,' John pointed out the obvious, 'frankly I am not at all comfortable with it. We havn't a clue what this place is, and the sooner we get out of here and leave it to others to study the better I shall be pleased. We've done our bit in finding it,' he added.

But we didn't leave.

'I wonder what happens if we follow the arrow?' I suggested, 'I bet nothing happens, after all what can?'

No one moved or spoke, they were still stunned by the flashing crack.

`We're all still here, and unharmed - we can leave when we like, so what's the problem?'

I was working hard to convince them, but I was really trying to convince myself.

`It seems harmless enough,' argued John, `but if you think it's OK then you go first, eh Ron? For me I'd rather stay here and watch and make notes.'

`It may be along time, if ever, before anyone else is here, so don't we owe it to our supporters as well as ourselves to find out all we can about the place?'

`OK then - off you go, we'll just stand by to pick up the pieces.' this from John.

I had made my mind up.

`Right,' I said, `here I go. Tell my mother my last thoughts were of her.'

No-one spoke, I think they thought this last comment was in poor taste.

And so I strode over to the `start' end of our half's arrow, and ignoring the crude red cross, began to walk slowly but deliberately along it. I reached its head without mishap but I was still on our side of the crack. I looked back to see they were all now standing and giving me every ounce of their attention.

I waved gaily with false confidence, turned and strode over the strange crack. Once on the other side I turned and looked back. Nothing happened and no-one moved, so I walked over to one of the stone seats and sat looking across at them.

The place was silent. We waited.

At first nothing happened.

I started to relax - prematurely.

Then as I gazed across I became gradually aware that whilst I watched, the other four started to look what I can only describe as `thin'. They were ever so slowly growing insubstantial. Soon I could see the background through them, and then some moments later they were gone.

Gone -

And I mean gone, there was nothing or no-one there, I was looking at a completely empty chamber.

I fought back the panic that was starting to grip my heart, and tried to get up and return across the crack - but I couldn't move. It was not that I had lost the willpower, but all my muscles were rigid. It was not just that I was unable to move but I found that I had no physical sensations. It felt as though I was totally insubstantial, simply not there. I had no physical presence whatsoever.

Worse - I was stuck there on the other side off that infamous crack, and now frighteningly on my own.

I remember that I badly wanted to cry. Why the hell had I decided to do this - I should have left it to one of the others.

Then, although I have no idea how long I remained paralized, there began a tiny change in the atmospheres in the other half. On the very edge of detection the air where each of the others were when I had last seen them seemed to get ever so slightly thicker. Very slowly shapes of see through people could be made out. These gradually became more and more substantial until it was clear that there, in the very same positions as before the strangeness began, were my companions. As I watched them re-appear I became aware that my sensations had returned and I could move.

God, was I thankful.

`There you are,' I said, `I don't know what happened then but we seem to be OK?'

It was a question.

Bill answered. `Yes, but where did you go? You completely disappeared.'

`And so did you, ' I replied.

`Well we all seem to be here now, let's not take any more chances until we have had a chance to discuss what goes on here, I for one don't like it.'

To which we all agreed.

But it was during this conversation that I realized that not all was as it was before. It was not obvious. Something incredibly subtle. Something in the quality of the voices perhaps or something in what I was seeing. Or was it a tiny time delay between sight and sound. Whatever it was I could not pin it down.

`Any-one else like to join me?' I asked.

To which there was a resounding `No thank you.'

But the strangeness did not end there.

I marched back over the crack along the other arrow from its heel to its head. Once I was wholy on the other side, back as it were with my friends I was suddenly frozen again, and shockingly the earlier process was repeated.

`What the heck was that?' Bill asked when they were all seemingly back to normal, `you went again.'

`And so did you,' I replied.

At this and without another word the equipment was packed up and five very puzzled and anxious people made their way back to the outside world via the tunnel.

Once back in camp, evening meal over, we fell to discussing our recent experiences.

`Well,' I said, `there's one good thing, people will have to believe us because it will all be on the DVD recording.'

`I'm afraid not,' Beharn replied sadly, `when nothing happened I turned off the recorder, and in any case I couldn't move.'

`Then I say that we should each write up the experience in detail, otherwise we will not be believed.' This was agreed.

We also agreed to return to the chamber the next day having in the morning formulated an action plan.

It was not to be.

In the night there was a short but intense period of heavy rain. The next day, on reaching the ledge, we found the entrance was now blocked by a rock-fall. We couldn't even agree as to where it had been. Water had got into the GPS locator and it was out of commission.

Most of the group it seemed were rather relieved not to have to re-visit the infamous chamber of recent strange events.

***

The return journey began with the team in a sombre mood as they were filled in varying degrees with a sad feeling of failure. But they had a couple of days to spare, and as they each concentrated on their own fields of interest normal good humour soon returned. Their memories of the events in the chamber became diffused as un-refreshed memories are want to do.

***

On their return to the capital they found that somehow the press had got hold of the finding of the cave and they were cajoled into a televised press conference. Even through the difficulties of the hesitant translator it went badly. The press had seen it all before - mysterious caves, disappearing people, holes in the ground that spouted light.

The questions revealed the level of scepticism -

`Did you have drugs with you?' `You can't say where this marvellous cave is - your GPS was not working, convenient eh?' `Pretty strong that local wine eh?' `Perhaps you found treasure and are keeping it to yourselves?'

Their reports, when written some time later differed substantially from each other.

They were not believed by most of the people who studied them. But there were a couple of notable exceptions. The first of these was a lecturer from Santiago's university who although retired still attended from time to time to do some research of his own. His speciality was local history. As the team were on their return journey he intercepted them, read their reports, and then asked to see them again. They met at the university and face to face they described their experiences in the chamber. The old professor sat and thought for a while and then, as if just making up his mind, he told them that he had come across a record left at the university by an explorer from many years before. What he had written was remarkably similar.

He said that the man had recorded what he thought the chamber was - but this was written in a local and very ancient form of Spanish for which unfortunately there was no direct English equivalent, the nearest the professor could tell them was that the explorer called the chamber by the words - `The place of the other same.'

This just added to the puzzle, and was unfortunately forgotten.

Back in the UK the press again were quickly on to the story and a TV news team persuaded them to take part in an interview with a well qualified but indifferent professor. Although the atmosphere was more polite and the questions more subtle the outcome was much the same. They left the studio very down hearted and retired to a nearby pub to convince each other that their experiences had been real.

This interview did trigger many expeditions from various eminent universities and explorers world wide to re-locate the chamber, but to this day it has still not been found.

But what of the members of the team? Who knows. After that punishing TV interview they separated, and each pursued their own discipline, these individuals, the only humans on record to have experienced what they did were almost immediately swallowed up in life's more normal routines, lived thereafter normal lives none of which was worth the attention of the rest of the world. Today they would probably be famous. It is not even known if any of them met again, after all the only thing they had in common was their recent history. History of a rather dubious, hard to credit, kind.

But then, at the time, there was at least one other individual who accepted the reports as fact. This rare and unbiased person was a notable British physicist of a high reputation and of some considerable fame. He obtained and read the team's records of the events. He then put his keen mind to the problem, separately interviewed each member of the team, and developed and published a well argued theory backed up by some sound science suggesting just what had been going on in inside that chamber.

It was, he said, a unique and extremely important place.

It was in fact, almost certainly, the only place on this planet where two separate universes met. Further, he proposed that the team member by crossing over that continuous crack, had travelled from this universe to a parallel one and back again.

He further suggested that the chamber had been visited before in some earlier era and fearing their experience these previous visitors had tried to warn any future explorers of the possible risks by scratching the red crosses on the arrows. An even earlier people, he thought, had made the arrows and inscribed the floor probably with names they had invented for each universe. It was, he argued, likely that the tunnel in the second half of the chamber led out into the other universe. Somehow, and at some time, their knowledge had been lost in the dust of the distant past.

And he had a warning; he declared that it was most fortuitous that none of the team had inadvertently changed anything, like dropping some item whilst `on the other side'- in which case they may not have been able to return.

Of course now, fifty years on, we know that his theory was correct in all respects. The team had unknowingly visited an alternative universe parallel to this one, a unique experience, and they had been fortunate to have survived.

JML
24/8/2008

INTIMACY DEFERRED

*H*e approached the door as he always did with a fast beating heart and a certain reverence, as one might when about to enter a grand cathedral. But this was no building to honour any deity, it could hardly be more mundane - it was in fact the local library. It was also where he first saw her, and he knew she would be there today. The automatic door swished open at his approach and he entered with every one of his senses tingling with anticipation. And there she was behind the long counter dealing with a small boy who was clutching the book he wanted to borrow. He simply stood there just inside the entrance as the door swished back into place, and gazed helplessly at her. To say he was in love is probably an understatement, she had stolen his heart and his soul.

Clark Longehope had made up his mind. This day it would be different, instead of simply indulging in idle banter as she logged his books - he would ask her to dine with him on a day of her choosing. He had wound himself up to do this being fearful that she would turn him down, he more than half expected it. He knew that she liked him from her smile, but was it enough? After all she smiled at all the customers.

All he knew about her was that her first name was Ellen, and that as librarian she was behind the desk from Monday to Thursday and half day on Friday, and that was all.

On this occasion it took him longer than usual to choose his new books, he found it difficult to concentrate, and once found himself clutching 'Knitting for Baby' and quickly returned it to the shelf after a queer look from a rather prim looking lady borrower.

Eventually he approached the check out point with his selection, but found himself in a short queue with other would be borrowers both in front and behind him. This was not in his plan. Clearly eager to deal with everyone efficiently she did not give him any chance to do that which he had determined to do. So after she had stamped his books instead of making for the exit he hung about pretending to read the notices. Again he got a strange look as he found himself avidly studying a leaflet which asked 'Do you think you are pregnant?'

It was approaching closing time, and he had been there for nearly three hours when at long last his chance came.

So he made his way nervously back to the counter - and Helen.

'Er, excuse me?' He began politely, ' but could I possibly have a private word with you?' He said, and nearly fainted as she looked directly into his eyes.

'Yes, of course, is everything all right?' She asked with concern.

'No........., I mean yes, that is er.......,' he hesitated, and then with a rush, 'would you like to have dinner with me? Any day you care to choose.'

At last he had done it, and he waited for her expected `Thank you, it's most kind of you, but no. I don't think my boy-friend would approve.'

Her worried look slowly gave way to that glorious smile. But still she hesitated as if weighing him up.

Then -

`I would like that very much, and I think Friday would be nice, it's my half-day,' This said slowly and with some hesitation. He was so taken aback that he was at a loss for words. He simply stared at her his features slowly breaking into a wide grin. Then he couldn't help himself,

`Blimey, that's great, I'll call for you by taxi at about seven - OK?'

And he started for the door.

`Yes, but don't you need to know where I live?' She called after him.

He turned red faced.

She laughed at his discomfort, quickly wrote the address on a piece of paper, and handed it to him with another heart stopping smile.

`Thank you,' he was all he could find to say, and made it to the door where he turned to give her a wave but she was already dealing with the another customer. He felt light headed, almost drunk with happiness,

***

In actual fact it was not his local library, that one had been recently closed by the council in a money saving series of cuts. It was simply the next nearest and Clark had been attending there now for about a year.

He lived on the other side of the city's busy suburbs but was a keen enough reader to make the forty-five minute bus journey to `her' library to change his books every two weeks or so. Nor, to be precise was it her library, she was an employee of the county's library service. She was a librarian. This duty she shared with two others, and as the library was not available every day, he did not see her on some visits.

Clark was not a young man, he was in fact middle aged. But he was a young middle age having so far led a quiet but very active life. As a regular attendee of the gym he sported a trim figure, tall, muscular and very masculine. With curly hair, expressive features and a ready smile he turned many a head when in female company. He now lived on his own having inherited his parents house when some years ago his mother had succumbed to cancer and his father had then given up all interest in living and had simply wasted away. He had a rather poorly paid job in his local bank.

Somewhat shy he was unused to female company having spent his earlier years looking after both parents during their infirmity, and had so far avoided the occasional attempts by female customers to get him interested in them having developed a range of polite strategies to put them off, and as we shall see there was little chance of his getting caught. He was therefore a comparative rarity, he was that is, a completely inexperienced older man, not just unmarried but also untested in the field of physical love.

He was therefore quite surprised at his recent boldness with the lovely Helen, and as the day of the dinner approached he became dreadfully worried that it would all go wrong and their relationship would end before it had begun. He had nightmares in which he succeeded in making a fool of himself as a result of which Helen would storm out after telling him never to activate the automatic doors of the library again.

His bank colleagues found themselves having to correct his work more than once, and grew concerned that something terrible had him in its grip. How surprised they would have been should they have divined the cause, that one of cupid's arrows had found its mark, impossible with old Clarky.

Inevitably the day arrived. Sensibly he had taken an over-due day off. But he was not at ease. Unable to concentrate on anything, he simple wandered about his house aimlessly twitching ornaments first this way then that, his mind in an increasingly fraught turmoil.

Carefully dressed, he had changed the shirt three times and his tie four, Clark jumped when the door chimes rang out announcing the arrival of his taxi. For the umpteenth time he checked that he had everything, cards, money, keys, hanky, and of course the all important address, to which she had thoughtfully added her surname Deffer, and her telephone number.

He left the house and was about to enter the cab, when -

'Don't you think you should shut your house door, Sir?' The driver asked politely.

Not a good start he thought as he ran back up the drive to comply.

Afterwards he could remember nothing of his journey to Helen's home, his mind was in a kind of spin. But eventually they arrived, and he strode purposefully up the neat garden path that belonged to a small terraced house, and pushed the door bell quickly before he could change his mind and run for it.

The bell was not answered immediately, and he was about to press it again when the door opened and there she stood looking puzzled at him standing there with one arm raised as if giving a royal salute.

There she was - cool perfection in a gown of some soft and clingy material, blue - green, the exact colour of her eyes.

`Hallo,' she said, `you're dead on time, I like punctuality. Are you all right?' She added.

Clark suddenly realized that he was still standing there with his mouth open.

`Er, yes - the taxi's waiting for us, shall we go?'

`That's the general idea,' she said and linking his arm gently propelled them towards the waiting car.

Nervous of each other they spoke little on the way.

`You look lovely,' he managed.

`Why thank you sir,' she replied with false formality. Then, `You look nice yourself.'

Not used to compliments, he did not know how to respond.

And then they arrived.

***

The meal was a great success. They quickly found that they shared many interests including wild life, walking, gardening, just being out of doors, and of course - books.

As they chatted on, happy to agree on almost every topic, there was just one in which he could not follow her. It was merely mentioned in passing as it were and it made no impression on him at the time - but it was a difference that was to have a tragic impact on their relationship.

`I usually attend church on Sunday, I always have,' she said.

`That's nice,' he replied, `unfortunately I stopped going some years ago, you're lucky to have that.'

And that was all - for the moment.

The meal was excellent, the wine just right, and the end of the evening found a very contented pair. If Helen had any doubts it was about Clark being so much older than she. If he had any it was that she was so much younger than himself.

He saw her to her door and she allowed him a quite long and soft kiss on the lips - definitely a lover's kiss.

As you may guess Clark was instantly transported onto another plane of existence. His life would never be the same again.

He had learned a great deal about Helen in that short time and he liked everything he heard. He now had an aim in his life, an objective, something to really look forward to and to put his energies into. A purpose.

We can but have every hope for him, poor Clark, he had picked an apple from the wrong tree. A good apple, sound and ripe, tempting, but just out of reach.

**

And so it was that Helen and Clark started dating. That is they met regularly for walks in the surrounding countryside, for meals and for an occasional visit to the theatre when something of mutual interest turned up. These occasions were looked forward to, and much enjoyed by both parties.

However, after some months their relationship had somehow not got any closer. Helen permitted the occasional kiss, but somehow by the whole attitude of her body managed

to make it very clear to Clark that it was as far as she would
allow him. She was no prude, she said, but it was not as if they
were committed or anything.

She paid many a visit to Clark's house, and on these
occasions made it plain that it would never be her choice, she
could not possibly live there.

`It's all right, I suppose,' she would begin, `but it's very old-
fashioned, I would want to change the whole place from top
to bottom.'

`What kind of a place would you be happy in?' He asked
curiously.

`I would like something modern but with potential, so
that I could finish up with a place that reflected me, not just
anyone.'

Clark had wondered many times why she had never invited
him over to her place. She seemed able to detect when the
conversation was moving in that direction and skilfully avoided
the issue.

He noticed this.

Helen had told him that like him her parents had passed
on and she lived in their house which she rented from the
council.

But to it he was not invited. She even actively discouraged
his questions as to what it was like inside. She insisted that
they always meet at his house or some mutually agreed neutral
building.

A year in and Clark was getting desperate, and after much
careful thought decided to propose to Helen. A very big step for
Clark this was. Money was still tight, but he had been saving
hard and he bought a ring.

They were at his house. `I have something very important to ask you,' Clark began.

Helen gave him that glorious smile and looked suitably expectant.

`Will you marry me?' He asked, at the same time bringing the little box out of his pocket.

And whatever he expected it was not to hear her laugh gaily.

`Where would we live?' She asked, `I certainly couldn't live here, and my place is much too small.'

Cleverly, this was not a `no' but nor was it a `yes'.

Poor old Clark did not now what to make of this. `Tell me what I have to do,' he said.

`For a start, I would need a place that I could live in,' she said. `What's for tea?'

And that for now was that. He returned the ring in its unopened box to his pocket.

So, with her words in mind he took her house hunting, and of course every place she chose was wildly outside his available price range. But taking her interest for encouragement he pressed on.

Then after many more months at last they found a place that she said `had potential' and was just within his financial capability.

Now frustration was beginning to eat away at Clark, he still felt the same overwhelming desire for Helen, but whenever he tried anything physical she would say `Please love, not yet, not until our relationship has been blessed by the church.'

`Which will be when?' he would ask.

`You know very well my dear, when we have somewhere to live.'

So, he gathered his resources together and having sold his own house he proceeded to buy the house that she had said `had potential.'

If he had thought that this would give him unlimited access to her body - he was mistaken. When on an occasion he managed to get his hand inside her clothing she ever-so-gently removed it, saying `Not yet, my love I couldn't sit in church on Sunday, please wait until after the ceremony.' Said so sweetly that he merely complied.

He had no choice but to begin the changes to the house that she said would be needed if she were to live there.

Inevitably this took up all his time and they began to see something less of each other.

A year later when the kitchen had been completed they celebrated.

But yet again Helen discouraged close physical contact. Clark had to be content with just a warm kiss.

`Now what we need to do to the living room is - ' and she reeled off the changes that she said were essential.

The work on the house kept Clark extremely busy, as you might imagine, leaving him precious little time for Helen. But worse was when she pointed out that the work stopped when she was with him and so she started to stay away on just those few precious days that had been their regular get-togethers. Now he had still never seen inside the house where she lived, and suggested more than once that she invite him in, but she usually said that it was much too untidy for such an important guest, promising another time, said with that innocent smile. But then he began to wonder what she did when they were apart, and he considered many times sneaking round when he was supposed to be working on the house. But he was afraid someone who knew them both might just see him and innocently mention it to her.

He wondered too about her parents. She had told him that a few years ago they had retired and had gone to live in Spain, and sure enough she did take a flight out once or twice in the year, but refused point blank to have him deliver her to, or collect her from the airport.

***

So what were these two mutually involved people really like? Well Clark was something of a dreamer, an optimist. He trusted people and expected them to have the same sound principles as himself. A caring nature caused some of his friends to think of him as a softy. But he had a steely strength under that easy going image. Clark was no fool. He should simply not have fallen for Helen.

As for Helen, she smiled a great deal, was a woman of the world who understood men. Her mother had brought her up to respect the church which they both attended every Sunday without fail, a duty with which Helen continued after her mother died.

Her father had deserted them when Helen was only ten years old. Her soft and gentle features would occasionally harden into a look of grim determination if she thought she as not being observed.

And Clarke began to wonder about her. It was almost as if she led a life from which he was excluded most of the time.

Nevertheless, love and optimism drove him on.

However, with Clark's limited resources, and the fact that he was not getting any younger, it took a further two years before they celebrated the completion of the living room.

She continued to promise a closer relationship when they had been blessed by the church. But to Clark their wedding was as far away as ever.

It took Clark two more years for the master bedroom.

Then the other two bedrooms, the lounge, the conservatory-And so on.

And then there was the garden.

On each successive achievement Clark would try to make love to Helen who would immediately bring in her church to defend herself, and then invent yet more changes to what she had come to call `our house'.

During all this time their meetings had grown even more sporadic, often he would not see Helen for a couple of weeks or more. Although now well past retirement age, a benevolent bank management let him stay on `for his knowledge and expertise' although the latest technologies had long ago left him behind.

***

Then, one sad day, Clark was over reaching himself at the very top of his tallest ladder to get at some remote corner with the paint roller, when for want of a younger man's sense of balance - he fell.

The fall was not immediately fatal, but had caused him some serious damage for which he was hospitalised.

Helen only came to see him once and unnerved by the elderly man he had now become did not return. Distressed by this turn of events Clark went downhill fast and died without his lovely Helen.

Clark's friends and colleagues who attended his funeral were somewhat surprised that Helen was absent. One week later they were even more surprised to read in the local paper that a certain Helen Deffer was to marry a Mr Ian Reddy - to whom she had been unofficially engaged for the last five years. One of Clark's workmates met Helen in town by accident and couldn't help but ask her why she had still led Clark on giving him to believe that one day she would be his. Her reply stunned him in its brevity -

`I didn't want to hurt his feelings, besides I was all he had,' she explained.

***

Now the one thing on Helen's mind was the house, `their' house, the one she knew would be hers and which she needed to sell if she and Ian were to live the way they had planned. As reported in the local rag the coroner found that Clark had suffered an accident and injuries from which he had subsequently died, it also named Clark's solicitor. So she phoned Goodwill and Grace and asked them if Clarke had left a will and when would the reading of it take place. She was asked what was her interest in Clark's will, and succeeded in convincing the secretary that she should be present on the day, and was duly given the information.

`Good old Clarky,' she said to Ian as she lay in his embrace relaxed and satisfied, `I knew he would do the right thing - he was like that, trustworthy. I could trust him with anything at all. We should be OK my love.' And she kissed him.

And the day of the reading arrived.

She was shown into Mr Grace's large office by the secretary. Mr Grace who was younger than she had expected quickly stood, bowed slightly to her, introduced himself and pointing to a chair near the back of the room asked her to please be seated. Next he apologised for the likely delay without relating the reason.

He then proceeded to ignore Helen and started to study some documents he picked up from his desk, whilst stopping now and then to write a note in the margin. Time ticked by and after about ten minutes she was about to ask the reason for the wait when Mr Grace looked at his watch and said, almost to himself, `Bang on time I bet.'

A gentle knock on the door and in came the secretary with a well dressed, attractive girl of about twenty.

Mr Grace stood again. `How are you my dear,' he said, `its very nice to see you again, I trust you had a pleasant journey.'

More pleasantries were exchanged which Helen noted were not accorded to herself. `What the hell's going on?,' she thought and, `who the devil is this girl?'

Mr Grace was not about to waste any more time, and without bothering to introduce the two women, began -

`Clark Longhope did indeed leave a will, which he signed, and is properly witnessed, and dated,' here he quoted the date, `and as far as I am aware he made no other.' He looked up at Helen who shook her head.

`So, as you already know,' he nodded to the girl, `Clark Longhope left his whole estate, including a house at......,' here he read out the address of the place Helen was used to call ours, `.........to his natural daughter Anne Longhope, that is to say you my dear,' this last directly to he girl.

Then pointedly to Helen..............

`No-one else is mentioned.'

JML
22/8/2008

THE LAST WORD

*V*ery, very gradually he began to be aware of himself. It was as if he was just waking up from a deep sleep. But that was all. There was nothing, absolutely nothing else, no surroundings, no up or down, no colour, and worse - no feeling of his physical self. In fact now he came to think of it he had no past and could not even recall his own name.

The only conclusion he could come to was that he must be in a hospital and was just about to regain consciousness. Then suddenly he had a name - Laurence Ian Edwards and he also knew that his friends called him Ly for short. But where on earth was he?

He next realised that he was travelling quite fast, at the wheel of a car in fact, along familiar streets and familiar surroundings.

This was a considerable shock, and he stopped just in time to avoid running into the rear of the lorry in front which was halted waiting for the lights to change. This situation, the one in which he had just become aware was frightening. What had he been doing? Had he fallen asleep whilst driving? He knew this could happen - but he was not tired and in all respects felt awake and fully alert. However it then occurred to him that he knew that he was a good driver and was heading for home.

- `HOME' he thought where in hell was it? All that was blank. It was not as if he had forgotten it, rather that there was just nothing there. A blank.

What was happening to him defeated all logic, he could make no sense of it whatsoever.

But strangely he knew where he was heading and was driving there with confidence.

He knew the right turnings and it was as if the knowledge was being realised just ahead of his vehicle. I seem to have little choice, he thought, but to continue on hoping that it would all make sense soon.

For some time he was forced to concentrate on his driving, the traffic was dense and there were many stops and hold-ups, and it was during one of these enforced stops that he looked round the car, and there beside him on the passenger seat was a large leather brief case the contents bulging out from beneath its unfastened lid.

Thank heavens his documents were there safe and sound, and he knew that the contents were vitally important, even of world-wide importance. A very great deal of money was at stake, but just then he had not the slightest idea why.

His wife would be cross again, demanding his attention and complaining once again about his bringing work home with him.

- `HIS WIFE' he could see Marion clearly in his mind's eye, attractive but now at middle age beginning to look somewhat comely. Perhaps, he thought, she would have been happier had they been blessed with offspring but it had just simply not happened in the thirty or so years they had been together, the opportunity had simply by-passed them. But he knew they were reasonably contented in their own way.

As he drove these thoughts introduced themselves into his mind without his conscious control. It was as if his life was being built up from the inside, inside his mind?

Eventually he slowed, indicated and turned the car into what was a cul-de-sac on a rather posh looking housing estate and swished up the short drive of number seventeen which turned out to be a four bed-roomed modern detached house with a well kept look about it. It was clear that it had been well cared for, the closely cut lawn was surrounded by well tended flower beds full of colour at this time of the year.

- ` TIME OF YEAR' - he knew it to be early summer, but felt that he had only just learned this obvious fact.

He pulled up just in front of the double garage, it already housed his wife's little run-about, and sat there turning these recent events over in his mind. He came to only one conclusion - none of it made any sense at all.

It was beginning to frighten him.

What terrible trauma had he undergone to find himself here with more unknowns than knowns.

He began to concentrate his thoughts, and soon found that whilst at first he was not aware of a particular aspect of his life he only had to turn his mind to it for it to appear as if it had always been there.

-`HOLIDAYS' - for example. When he put his mind to a particular year he would gradually become aware of where they had been and even some of the things they had done.

But then it all changed.

He was not being allowed to remain there in his car trying to make sense of his situation. Some external force made him grab his brief-case, leave the car and searching his pocket for the door key, march up the drive, and turn the key in `HIS' front door to let himself in. And also without being able to prevent it, made him shout -

`Marion dear, I'm home at last.'

- `AT LAST' - what did he mean by that? Just then he had no idea.

He was made to wait at the bottom of the stairs as his wife appeared and smiled as she came down to meet him. It was clear that she had gone to some special effort to look her best, and he thought she really did look gorgeous, dressed in light flowing summer fabrics, her long light brown hair bouncing round her shoulders and with that familiar smile and that sparkle in her brown eyes.

What happened next was as natural as it was what he wanted. He picked her up in his arms and swung her around before planting a long kiss on those soft warm lips - and felt her respond, a promise for later he knew.

`Well dear was it the success you had hoped for? Did you have a good trip?' The questions asked in that special low voiced breathless way she had which never failed to thrill him.

`Yes to both,' he replied, `tell you all about it later.' He wondered what this meant as yet he had no recollection as to where he had been or why, but he did have a feeling as to its importance. BUT WHY DIDN'T HE KNOW?

`I'll run a bath for you whilst you have a drink you look as if you could do with one. I can have a meal ready by the time you come down - I suppose you have had enough of eating out. OK?'

`Great,' was all he could find to say, and kissed her again by way of filling the awkward gap.

Where on earth had he been, and just what had he been doing? He still had no idea.

He heard Marion turn on the bath water, and then make for the kitchen where she busied herself in the job of preparing a meal, `efficiently as usual,' he thought.

- `AS USUAL' the phrase came immediately to mind, but he had no recollection at all of any previous meals they had shared - but strangely shared he knew they had, often.

Whilst waiting for his bath, he wondered naturally into their spacious well appointed lounge, poured himself a large neat Glenmorangie and sat gratefully down into the comfort of his armchair.

- `HIS' armchair. `Here we go again how the devil did he know which was his, and his favourite scotch?' He thought hard but could come to no certain conclusion other that the harsh reality that he may have lost his memory which was being re-generated by the sight and feel of the familiar. But when and how did this happen? He had no idea and so far he was bereft of any clues. Just as he was going to panic Marion called to say his bath was ready.

It was while he was relaxing in the healing warmth of his bath it came to him that something or some-one was dripping information piece by piece as it was needed into his mind. The more he considered it, the stronger became the feeling that he was being manipulated by some agency outside his mind. Not prone to panic, nevertheless at this thought a terrible anxiety gripped him, and it took all his self control to keep from screaming. He was now quite desperate to get to the bottom of this ludicrous situation.

Dressed and bathed he found Marion seated in the other big chair nursing a pre-dinner gin and tonic.

She smiled at him and said, `Now, tell me all about it, there's time before we eat. Was it a good conference? Did you succeed? Did Henry give you his support?'

His mind was blank, at first that is. Then without any further thought he began -

`Yes it went well, several of the big drug companies have agreed to start trials, and if these workout OK we could be very rich. But it will take time - the patents have yet to come through and I won't release anything until after that.' He paused to absorb what he had just said, then, `I didn't see much of Henry Spears but I believe he was working wonders behind the scenes.'

So he knew a Henry Spears.

He now also knew that he had been in Florence attending a meeting of research managers of some of the worlds biggest companies engaged in the battle to conquer one of the planet's most serious health problems which caused a significant number of early deaths in the dense industrial populations and was steadily gaining ground.

For legal reasons we will call the problem simply `HTo' disease.

And he, Ly, had, he believed discovered a cure the bald facts of which he had been presenting - and it had gone very well indeed, much better that he had expected.

- `THAN EXPECTED' so his past was being introduced as well as the present, but only as it was required. He found he was unable to think the of past by means of his own contemplation.

He was none the wiser as to what was going on. Tiredness was overtaking him so he decided to ignore his situation for the moment and enjoy his dinner and the company of Marion.

In this his wife proved that she was sensitive to his mood and chatted lightly about her week whilst he had been away, and he learned quite a bit about their life together. It appeared that whilst there was no burning passion between them, they were nevertheless more than comfortable with each other. Marion had, it seemed, a circle of women friends who met regularly, shared small intimacies, and when required rallied round to help each other. Alice and Andrew Stabletown had been in the throes of a divorce and Alice was the latest to get the all girls together treatment in spite of the fact that most of the group blamed her for the break-up.

He was only required to listen, and an hour or so later after helping with the washing -up he pleaded the tiredness he really did feel, excused himself, kissed his wife, and mounted the stairs to his bedroom.

- `HIS' bedroom. But he could no longer absorb this new fact.

Sleep overcame him as his head hit the pillow.

But his slumber was broken by a vivid dream in which he was an author and was busy writing about himself, not autobiographically but as if he was another person.

Little did he know how prophetic this was.

***

The next few days were characterised by routine. Car to the laboratories. Work on a report of the conference for his boss and the directors. Overseeing the work in the labs.

And generally keeping the cure for HTo running to schedule.

Then the news broke.

The world press was on to it, and Ly was swallowed up in the melee of interviews for the papers and for television.

Huge fortunes were predicted if the final trials were a success. Rivalry between the drug companies was intense - the race was on.

It seemed that he would be able to demand his own salary.

Ly had little or no time to devote to the situation in which he had so recently discovered himself - as if from nothing and nowhere.

And there was another big problem, Ly was not happy with this career, successful though it was, he very badly wanted to be a writer. As far as he knew he had always wanted to write fiction - where people and situations were strictly under his control.

Then came a welcome break. Marion, aware of the strain the work was putting on him suggested a holiday away from it all. He readily agreed and she booked into a quiet hotel on the Scottish Island of Skye. It was now late October and the weather was warm and sunny - just what he needed. `Two weeks of this and I'll be a knew man,' he thought.

But he had no way of knowing how true this would turn out to be.

**

It was on the third day of this break when matters of his identity started to intrude again. Marion and he were relaxing on chairs on the hotel lawn with its superb mountain views. The sun shone from a cloudless sky, his Glenmorangie and her G and T were to hand.

Ly began to consider what he already knew of his life and thus started to identify some very awkward gaps. Had he any family? Or friends? Where was he educated? And even how old was he? Why did he not know these simple but important facts.

No matter how hard he concentrated the answers did not come.

But these considerations were short lived as he gradually became aware of a powerful force clamping firmly down on his mind. He was being prevented from asking those questions he was now so keen to ask. The source of this censorship seemed to be inside his own head, and yet he was certain that the agency was outside himself. And then it came to him as a terrible shock and with real certainty - his mind was under the rule of -

-`ANOTHER PERSON'.

It was a serious blow.

It would seem that he was not in full control of himself. So who, or what, was?

He was suddenly overtaken by a surge of debilitating panic. Sweat broke out on his now ashen face. He rose and began to walk round the lawn in an agitated, wild eyed manner. Marion ran to him and tried to calm him, but feeling that she was part of the conspiracy - he swore at her and she retired in tears. Disgusted with himself at this, he wandered away from the lawn, and taking a path through the trees soon found himself on a rocky outcrop overlooking the sea. There as he sat on a convenient stone the sound and movement of the sea gradually brought him calm.

After a while with mind a blank he then began a process of clear thinking.

`The first thing,' he thought, `is to accept that there was another person's mind inside my own head.'

Next - he contrived to convinced himself that he was not going insane.

He needed to develop a constructive plan, but a first step seemed obvious, it seemed therefore essential to make contact with this other individual, and establish his purpose in being there.

Meanwhile he would have to keep all of this to himself to avoid being locked up as a lunatic or at worst a dangerous schizophrenic.

How to begin?

Ask a question, but what question. The obvious one?

So concentrating his whole mind -

`Who are you?'

Nothing. A challenge then?

`If you don't answer me I'll throw myself off this cliff.' He tried hard to mean it, and slowly walked to the edge.

Then shockingly inside his head came -

I will not allow you to do such a silly thing, it would achieve nothing, I would merely start again.

`What on earth do you mean by start again?'

I am the Author and you are one of the characters in the book I am writing - but things seem to have gone wrong, it should not be possible for a writer to talk to one of his invented people. Although I must confess that they do sometimes take control of the story. By start again, I mean that I would simply tear up this piece and begin another leaving you out of it - you would simply disappear. Vanish.

This was a shocking revelation to Ly. He needed time to think.

`OK, I won't do anything stupid if you promise to leave me to my own devices until this time tomorrow - agreed?'

The Author also needed time to consider matters, as far as he was aware this kind of thing had never happened before.

***

Now as it happens the Author was a micro-biologist by training and had recently been made redundant at the ripe old age of forty and was finding it hard to get a job with any of the big drug cartels in spite of a good university degree and years of appropriate experience. So in order to bring in some much needed money he had turned his hand to writing and had already had a couple of novels published both of which were doing quite well. But he badly wanted to get back into industry, and his real ambition was to create a cure for some fatal condition like the notorious `HTo' disease. But unable to satisfy this ambition he had resorted to writing a story about a micro-biologist who did succeed in devising a cure. This person was non other than Ly, with whom even at this stage of the book he identified quite powerfully. He planned that Ly should be recognised world-wide as the finder of a cure for HTo, and that as a result he would become quite rich and even rewarded with a knighthood. However he recognised that this was only the bare bones of the story - the core in fact. He had not as yet worked out the other characters and their roles, but he had it in mind that life was not going to be kind to Ly, in fact he was destined for a sticky and unpleasant end. The Author decided to keep this intention from him.

In fact the more the Author considered this unlikely and ludicrous situation in which an author is able to communicate with his subject the more worried he became. Questions started to bubble to the top unbidden -

What if we cannot agree?

If I write him out will he re-appear in another book?

Perhaps I can't get rid of him - he might simply re-appear as another character? After all his only unique quality is that I can talk to him.

After a sleepless night he determined one thing, and that was he must somehow regain control of the situation, but how?

***

Ly on the other hand was equally at a loss. But in his case he was determined to sit tight and try not to provoke the Author into removing him.

He was so self absorbed, his features etched with tress as he faced his breakfast that Marion became seriously concerned. He was on the verge of panic and in spite of trying very hard to hide his fears from her, he failed miserably.

`What on earth is bothering you love, I have never seen you look so worried,' she said.

`Nothing dear,' he replied, `I'm afraid that the opposition will beat us to it.' In this he meant the Author, but as he intended she thought he meant the competition for a cure for HTo.

`I have total faith in you, I'm sure it will be all-right.'

And he knew these words to be the Author's.

He then, without being aware of any transition, found himself entering his spacious office. With a great effort of self control he took command - told his secretary he was not to be disturbed, and seated himself behind his desk where she had thoughtfully turned on his PC where it sat showing a screen saver of a peaceful ocean scene.

'What now?' He asked aloud and was immediately answered by that now familiar dread voice in his head.

'*Well, I was simply going to get on with the story,*' came the reply.

'What exactly does that mean for me?' He asked.

'*Well at this point you were about to be recognised as something of a hero for your discovery and to begin to reap the benefits of wealth and fame.*'

In this the Author deliberately failed to mention that it was all going to unravel and the future held pain and suffering for poor old Ly.

NOW - this was the point at which in this very strange situation something even more inexplicable happened.

LY FOUND THAT HE COULD SEE THE AUTHOR'S THOUHTS

He saw that what was intended for him was a distinctly unhappy future, but the detail was absent as the Author had not as yet determined it. He also saw that the Author was unaware of this new found ability of his.

Ly realised that in order to avoid what unhappy plans the Author may dream up for him, he - Ly, would have to take control.

BUT HOW?

Then with no better idea than to turn the tables on the Author, and summoning all his remaining mental strength, he turned to his computer keyboard and started to type as fast as he could, not a report, or a memo but the beginning of A STORY. It was his very first step on the road to his becoming A WRITER.

"Mark Standish was a microbiologist about to become famous as the inventor of a cure for the dreaded ailment THo." He wrote.

`How the blazes did you know my name? And that I was a microbiologist?' Asked the Author._

`Because it's the name I have given you,' Ly the Writer replied. He suddenly found just what it was like to be in charge again.

- He was REAL. - Alive, A proper person. He became aware of his past, and all the missing substance of his life. He was aware of himself. He was REAL - yes REAL. It was almost impossible to believe.

Then from somewhere in a remote part of his mind he barely heard the Author turned micro-biologist complaining-

`This isn't fair it is you who are supposed to be my character in my story not the other way round. It is me who is real not you. You can't do this to me - I am the Author.'_

But the Writer knew that Mark was merely the subject of his story about a micro-biologist, and looking round him he found that instead of his office he was now in his own box room at home where he had started to compose this story on his PC.

`Shall I bring you a cup of tea dear, or will you come down for it?' Marion called.

`Yes please,' he answered,`that would be great, up here please I'm parched.'

As she entered he thought just what a delightful and sexy woman he had the good fortune to marry. But before he could demonstrate his affection he had to get on with the story. He had to work fast he could still just hear that other voice although it was now so faint that he could only just make out the words with difficulty.

***

Ly's story to begin with dealt with Mark Standish's background. It was where his subject had returned from a successful conference that the mood of the story changed.

"The world's press was at his door and the drug companies were lined up to compete for the privilege of access to the patent." He wrote, and after a pause for thought continued -

"Partridges landed the job and they soon had a production line going, and at last the cure was available. At first nothing happened, not even a relief from the severely debilitating condition.

"Then things got worse - a number of other research organisations tried to repeat Mark's tests with catastrophic results. Test animals died in great pain and at Partridges individuals on the double blind tests became seriously ill.

"The press got hold of it and an investigation was called for, and was eventually agreed to by the company for which Mark was working. They found that when Mark did the experiment it worked but it failed when in other hands. What on earth was going on?

"The company appointed an independent group to look into the matter, and after an exhaustive search and subsequent detailed analysis they hit on the problem. They found that Mark had used his own blood in the culture used to test the efficacy of the drug. Tragically, Mark's blood type was an extremely rare one, less than one percent of the world's population had this type. After much further testing it was discovered that Mark's cure for HTo only worked for people with this same blood type. All other types gave an adverse reaction leaving the disease alive and fully functional.

"Unfortunately everyone was looking for a scapegoat, and in spite of the fact that Partridges should have discovered the problem before the trial with real people, it was easier and less damaging to pile all the blame onto the scientist in charge of the initial discovery, and that was Mark."

At this stage Ly began to feel sorry for the Author-cum-microbiologist but if he were to feel secure in his new found real world outside the pages of the story he had to be stern and write the bitter end.

It was as he had determined this, but hesitated before this final act, he heard a small voice in the back of his mind. It said -

`Please, I beg of you don't do this. What have I done to deserve it?'

Ly gritted his teeth, placed his hands over the key board and wrote -

"Mark's wife and two sons were unable to cope with the intense media pressure and were seriously considering moving away and leaving Mark to his fate. Then after a disastrous day in court Mark returned home to find his youngest son terribly ill. He was diagnosed as having contracted HTo.

"Mark blamed himself even though the safety procedures at the lab were practically contamination proof. A further problem was that his son's blood was plain type O.

"The day after his family left, Mark parked his car in the garage poked a piece of hosepipe into the car exhaust and into the car, shut the doors and sat back to listen to the sweet sound of the engine.

"He was found the next day by their jobbing gardener. It was all over."

Or was it?

As Ly wrote of Mark's funeral and had reached the point where the assembled friends and relatives had turned away from Mark's grave and were leaving, a voice as if from a long way off was clearly heard to say -

'Your story is at an end, but mine has barely begun - remember I am still the Author.'

JML
7/10/2008

SATISFACTION

*S*ophie's day dawned just like any other, but it was destined to change her life for ever.

Her husband Leonard was away on business so she was free to please herself how to spend her time, and she had it in mind to phone Ann, her closest friend and suggest leisurely shopping trip to town with lunch at their favourite pub. She was in no hurry and was taking a shower when the door chimes interrupted her thoughts. Thinking it was probably the postman with something requiring a signature she merely wrapped herself in a bath towel slipped her feet into her slippers and made her way downstairs.

She was startled to see standing on the porch step not the postman but a uniformed policeman and a police woman. In her surprise she clutched the towel round her. The man touched his helmet in salute, coughed, and in a gentle voice said, `Mrs Leonard Slyman?'

`That's me,' she replied, `What is it?'

`I'm very sorry, but we have some very bad news for you. May we come in?'

Shocked and mind in turmoil she showed them into the living room.

`Please sit,' she said. Then feeling vulnerable, `I must put some clothes on. I'll not be long.'

Whilst dressing she went over the possibilities, Leonard was in France and she had had her usual call from him the previous evening and he seemed on top form; so it couldn't be about him. She was at a loss to guess.

Both officers stood as she entered the living room. `I am sergeant Phil Green and this is constable Jill Ryan,' began the man. `I think you will need to be seated.'

They all sat and she waited.

`I am truly sorry to have to tell you that your husband Leonard Slyman was involved in a multiple car accident in France late last night and was found to be dead on the spot. I really am sorry.'

Sophie was stunned. How could this be? Leonard was an excellent driver and was used to driving in France.

`Please tell me what happened,' she managed.

The police woman stood, `Is that the kitchen through there? Can I make you a cup of tea?' She acknowledged Sophie's nod and left them.

`Is there anyone you would like to be here? The man asked.

`No thanks, later perhaps - please tell me what happened - all of it,' she added.

`Well, we don't know all the facts yet, but it appears that your husband was returning from a night out at a restaurant in the town of Nantes when his car was hit by a car or cars at an intersection. It is thought that at least three cars were involved and so far no one has been found alive. As far as I have been able to ascertain he was killed instantly and could not have suffered,' he paused to let her recover a little.

Eventually he continued, as the girl returned with a tray and three mugs of steaming tea, and milk and sugar.

`He is currently at the town hospital where he will remain until the inevitable police enquiries are complete. And you will be required to identify him, unless you can suggest anyone else.'

`I will do it, I suppose there will be arrangements to be made about bringing him back here,' Sophie replied.

Outwardly she had regained some composure, but inside she was utterly bewildered.

`OK,' said the man with some relief, no one liked these jobs.

`Would you like me to stay for a while?' The woman asked.

`No thank you very much,' she replied.
And they left.

***

Ann proved a good friend and spent quite a bit of time with her giving her support and assisting with the essential arrangements.

Leonard had always ensured that she had a small bank account of her own so she could organise her inevitable trip to France without having to go through Leonard's solicitor. She had no worry about expenditure as she assumed that the house they had lived in for the last thirty years, its contents and any other assets would be hers.

Her first shock was when the solicitor told her that there was no will, Leonard had died in testate. Worse he had only recently taken the will he had previously drawn up and had destroyed it.

What was going on?

Her nice comfortable world was crumbling.

She then had two more devastating shocks in quick succession.

Leonard had always looked after the money side of their relationship, which had seemed right with him being the sole bread winner. This he did from the `quiet' room he called his study where he sat at his big desk, `to do the accounts,' he said.

Sophie couldn't find a key so she broke open the desk with a knife.

It did not take her long to discover the worse.

There was the bank account with the last statement only days ago, and instead of the life savings she had expected there was just a few tens of pounds - it had all been withdrawn the previous month. All one hundred thousand pounds of it.

Underneath the bank statement she found a building society account to the effect that a mortgage had been agreed for almost the full value of their house.

As the shock wore off she began to cry. It was not just that she was broke and no longer owned the house - but she had been so cruelly deceived.

Then she started to get angry.

What the hell was Leonard playing at? - where the devil was all this money?

She tackled the solicitor but he couldn't or wouldn't tell her anything relevant except a hint that Leonard had enquired about moving large amounts of currency abroad - perhaps to France.

The arrangements for her visit to France were complete and before she left she had time to reflect on their past.

They had been childhood lovers, and their earlier marriage years were idyllic by any standards. True they had no children but this had not seemed to matter as they were engrossed in each other. Leonard's job was well paid and as a senior representative for a large drug company he was often required to spend time at the headquarters which was sited near Nantes in France.

But as Sophie considered matters she began to admit to herself that recently their relationship had not been as active it once had been, and that Leonard had been to France without her many more times in the last couple of years.

And a deep suspicion began to grow in her mind. Just what had this husband that she no longer knew been up to. Her resentment towards him began to replace a lifetime of love and affection, and of course trust.

Sophie determined to find out.

**

Once in France Sophie's first call was to the company's headquarters. Here Leonard's boss, who spoke perfect English, could not have been more charming or sympathetic, and whilst he helped her where he could, he knew nothing of his employees financial affairs.

He did however mention a local solicitor to whom the company had been notified to send any legal correspondence.

Sophie's knowledge of French was almost nil, so making an appointment with the solicitor was difficult but she managed it. In the meantime she had to call at the police station where they would take her to identify her husband.

The police found someone to translate and she learned that he had been returning home from a party, when at a junction a drunk had walked out into the road and in trying to avoid him three cars had hit each other and all occupants had been killed.

And in answer to her question - No, there was no one else in Leonard's car.

As she looked at the dead Leonard it was as if she did not know him. Her heart was ice in her breast - all she could think was that if there was no money they could do what they liked with him, and be damned.

As she gazed at him she thought he looked to have shrunk. Not handsome in the conventional way, he had in the past attracted many an admiring glance from the opposite sex. But that was then, and now he was here dead on a cold slab.

*

The taxi dropped her off at the solicitors.

At the front desk she simply stated her name and was immediately shown upstairs and the receptionist waved Sophie to wait whist she knocked and went in.

The door opened and Sophie was waved into a very large room with one very big desk behind which sat a rather stern looking man dressed in an old fashioned dark suit and wearing a pair of half moon spectacles. The walls of the room were a clutter of shelves, books, and folders bound with tape. It had an air of dusty years about it.

The receptionist stood by the desk and with poor English helped to translate.

But to the surprise of Sophie in one of the two chairs facing the big desk and turning to look at her with some curiosity was an extremely good looking blonde girl of about half Sophie's age.

The solicitor nodded for her to take the other chair and she sat.

He then introduced the other woman as a mademoiselle Cloie Le-Strange, and then introduced her to the girl.

In slow French he then addressed the girl. She was it seemed there to claim her inheritance from Leonard, All of what he had - the bank account and the house at Simonville plus its furnishings and the paintings.
Sophie sat up.

The house at Simonville and contents - it was beginning to make a kind of horrible sense. She knew with absolute certainty that this is where all the money and the house in England had gone. And she was about to loose it all to Leonard's mistress - this mere slip of a girl.

Rage engulfed Sophie, it was not aimed at this girl but at Leonard - how could she have missed what had been going on under her nose for who knows how long. Then these sentiments were interrupted as the solicitor began again. It seemed that he was asking the girl if she had any written proof of Lionel's intention to leave it all to her.

When he paused the girl exploded in a speech of rapid French which with much waving of her arms went on for some time. The receptionist tried to translate.

`Why do I need proof ---- everyone knows he loved me ---- he said it many times ---- only right after what I was to him ----- where's the justice ----- now I have not got him what am I to be left with if not his money?' And much more of the same. She then turned to Sophie and thrusting her head close to Sophie's `He was going to marry me,' she screamed, it was all arranged.' and she burst into tears.

Not knowing how French justice worked Sophie feared the worst - the girl seemed to have a good case.

When the girl had finally worn herself out the solicitor turned to Sophie and asked quietly if she could produce her certificate of marriage to Leonard Slyman, perhaps in the next two weeks or so.

`Qui monsieur,' Sophie replied with the only French she knew.

`Bon,' he replied, and slowly so that the receptionist would make no mistake told her that he would arrange for her to visit the property which was now hers and to have the bank account transferred into her name. This brought a tirade of abuse from the girl who was ushered out still loudly protesting by the receptionist.

When they had left the room the solicitor looked up at her over his glasses, smiled at Sophie, and said in clear English - `Mrs Slyman, I am truly sorry for your husband's death, and for subjecting you that ordeal, but I trust that you will find some compensation in the house. I know of it. It is quite charming and in a lovely spot. I am sure you will fall in love with it and I hope that you might one day come here to live where I think you will find you will be made most welcome. If you have any problems please come to me, I will be in touch.' With that he stood and held out his hand to indicate the interview was over.

**

The house proved to be everything Sophie could have wished for, and with the sea visible beyond its pretty garden it was simply perfect. With Leonard's funeral well behind her she invited Ann over for a prolonged stay.

One beautiful spring evening they were sitting in the garden sipping from glasses of local wine and enjoying the absolute peace of the place when Ann asked her how she felt about things now.

She thought for a while and then said -

`Satisfaction.

`Satisfaction that I have the money we both contributed to.

`Satisfaction that I have this lovely place to live in.

`Satisfaction that his mistress got nothing in the end.

`But above all, satisfaction that he died just in time.'

JML
14/12/2008

STRIKE

*J*eremiah was hauled dripping wet and more than half drowned from Sydney harbour. Unable to swim he was extremely fortunate to survive at all. He was spotted falling from one of her majesty's naval vessels and grabbed roughly by a tall, wiry, but powerful man, lifted easily from the water and dumped in an untidy heap on the deserted harbour quay. After he had coughed up most of the bay he had swallowed, his rescuer helped him to his feet and took a long cool look at him.

'Can you speak for yourself mate?' The man asked.

'Yes, sir,' the lad replied.

'Then what in God's name were you doing to fall from yonder ship, eh lad?'

'I won't go back there - no matter what,' the boy stated, and it was clear to the man that he meant it.

'Then you had best come along with me,' the man said.

And as the boy seemed to have little choice in the matter - he did.

Jeremiah was of course not his real name. Christened William Shanks back in England he had sense enough to adopt another lest 'they' came looking for him.

As it was he had been seen by one of the ship's hands to fall from the high deck, at which point he was lost sight of in the murky harbour waters. At a later official naval enquiry he was taken to have drowned, his body having been washed out to sea. In due course his mother was informed by means of a formal naval letter which told her that he had given his life honourably whilst loyally serving his ship. Bill worried how his mother and his young brother were managing without him. He felt certain that he would never see them again. He was never going back to that place - never. But unknown to Bill his mother's grief was short lived since as a victim of her needs she had set her sights on, and had already married another working man.

So how did this nearly drowned Lancashire lad find himself in Australia?

When his father died three years ago a very young Bill Shanks had found himself the sole breadwinner with his job at one of the bleak North England's many dark mills. He was poorly paid as a `reel boy' responsible for keeping the machine minders supplied with full reels. His father had succumbed in one of the many outbreaks of influenza which decimated the families living crushed together in mean back to back terraced houses. Only the foul un-swept street where the sunlight rarely reached separated the rows of gloomy dwellings, and being so close upon each other the whole neighbourhood was afflicted. They only just survived, the three of them, his Mother, his two year old brother and himself.

Back there, trouble when it came would be swift and conclusive.

There had been a break-in at the mill owner's big house and valuable items were stolen. Too hot to handle they had been cursorily hidden nearby to await the hullabaloo dying down. One night after work had finished for the day Bill was exploring a nearby derelict house, looking, he later said, for anything he might use or sell. Under some old sacking he lit upon the booty and was caught on the spot grasping a silver candle holder. His protests were unheeded and at his trial he was found guilty of house breaking and given the choice of either one month in prison or serving on one of the navy's ships of war for a minimum of one year. Thinking that he was unlikely to survive prison he chose to take his chances with the navy. So without being allowed to say goodbye to his mother he was dumped in a wagon with several other miscreants and a couple of tough looking guards and bounced and bumped to the Liverpool docks.

Here he was escorted with three other men up the waiting gang plank onto the deck of a towering fighting vessel where the boson and a couple of hefty sailors waited for them. He was assigned to the boson and almost immediately with the shouting of many incomprehensible orders the ship got under way. They were at sea for several weeks. Bill's knowledge of the world was almost nil. He was staggered at the immensity of the oceans which seemed to go on for ever, indeed his whole tiny world had suddenly expanded into this limitless space of nothing but sea and sky. And the winds which drove the ship now assumed an ever present importance. The work was hard and equally exacting but the contrast with what he had been used to could not have been greater. Billy knew his life had changed for ever, and the excitement of it filled his heart and his mind.

Apart from a couple of stops in foreign ports to pick up supplies during which he was kept a close eye on, he found himself in Sydney harbour.

Little caring where he was he determined to jump ship, the unknown seemed to him to be better than the knotted rope's end the boson all too frequently wielded. Then seizing an opportunity when the boson's attention was otherwise engaged he scaled the side timbers and jumped for dear life. He broke the surface and paddled and splashed the short distance to the quay, whilst the ship sailed on to its allotted mooring without him.

And so now, here he stood, his whole future in the hands of this stranger.

`What's ye name lad?' The man asked.

Billy paused for thought. All he knew was bits of the Bible, it would have to do.

`Jeremiah Saul,' he said.

The man said nothing as he looked at Billy, a smile taking over his rugged features, the smile became a grin, and the grin a loud and long guffaw.

`Jeremiah's too long and too grand for the likes of you,' he said when he had recovered some composure, `so I think we'll call thee Jerry.

`And my name's Samuel, Sam Grains, but you call me Boss. All right?'

`All right,' replied Jerry with some relief. Things did not seem to be too bad - so far.

`And don't worry lad, ye'll soon be dry in this heat,' Boss told him.

They walked a short distance to where a horse and open wagon waited and Boss lifted him easily and dumped him on top of a pile of boxes and knobbly sacks, and they were off.

The first hazard was at the port gate where two uniformed men stood checking everything which was leaving. Jerry thought that this was the end of his short adventure but information about an escaped boy had not yet reached the guards, in fact it never did. And Jerry was reckoning without Boss.

Boss was evidently well known to the guards and after showing them a sheaf of documents he waved a hand towards the lad and said `I'd like you to meet young Jerry here he's my new farm hand. You'll be seeing more of him when he's learned the routine.'

`Hi Jerry,' said the guard with a friendly grin, `you've picked a good man there mate,' he nodded at Boss, and he waved them through.

And so Jerry's Australian adventure had begun.

***

A big bright yellow sun shone down on them as they rattled through the streets surrounding the harbour. Jerry, as we must now call him, stared with wide eyes at everything. Boss grinned as he watched the lad trying to take it all in at once. Jerry was mesmerised by the colours which everywhere splashed the scene. Used only to seeing dark red brick set in a dismal grey, this vividness almost hurt his eyes. And as they trotted through the suburbs he thought the people living here must be gentry so grand and beautiful were the houses. And tall buildings of light coloured stone made a lasting impression on him as he gazed at them open mouthed. It was then that he formed an ambition to live here one day in such a place of his own.

They soon left the houses behind and rattled and swayed along a wide road carved by the ruts of many a wagon. It was busy too as a variety of horse-drawn vehicles bounced along in both directions.

Jerry was mesmerised by all he saw and all too soon they turned off this broad highway onto a narrower track which wound its way by fields upon fields as far as the eye could see. Some fields had ripening crops, some had sheep, and some cattle, and many more were just green grass. As they drove Boss pointed everything out, and was glad to see that the lad took it all in. Every now and then they passed long low ranch houses and barns, and after a long couple of hours Boss turned off the track and pulled the horse to a standstill in front of one such building.

`Welcome to Bonshell Farm - our, and now your home,' Boss announced as they came to rest.

Suddenly they were surrounded by two small girls and a tall strong looking woman, all of whom gazed with undisguised curiosity at Jerry.

`This 'eres Jerry, our new hand,' said Boss, `and these are my wife Ruth and the girls Juney and Sue my uncontrollable daughters,' he added.

Jerry's first job was to help unload the wagon, watched by the giggling girls safely hiding behind the barn.

Next Boss showed him his quarters. The house had a separate lean-to building inside of which he was shown a sizable room well fitted out with table, chairs, and a formidably large sideboard. The room's other door led to a comfortable bedroom and a tiled bathroom.

`This will be yours,' Boss explained, `but you will be eating with us.' He added.

`I think you'll be comfortable enough.'

Jerry was speechless - all this for him - it did not seem possible.

Boss grinned at him taking pleasure in the lad's wonderment.

'Before we go any further,' he said his expression now quite stern.

'Conditions:' -

'Starting from now you will work under my strict instructions for one whole week and for this you will not be paid. At the end of the week we will review your work and if I like what I see I will employ you as a trainee farm hand, and you will be paid a wage. You will only take orders from me and no-one else. Do you agree?'

'Yes Sir,' Jerry managed.

'Boss - call me Boss, and first go and get a proper wash - you stink. Ruth, that is Mrs Grains, will bring you some clean clothes, and when you've done that come to the house for some grub, I'm starvin' and I'm sure you must be.'

And with this Boss turned and vanished into the house.

So Jerry was home. Oh yes - 'and dry'.

***

That first week for Jerry went in a flash. Boss kept him busy, and having shown him what was required he expected Jerry to pick it up first time. At the end of that week the thin straggly rather frail looking lad that was Jerry had begun to fill out. He was becoming bronzed and muscles wer beginning to show on thin limbs. Above all he was thoroughly enjoying himself, a fact that Boss noticed with pleasure. Jerry had never known such continous enjoyment in his life, and to cap it all Boss took him on and he had money of his own. Out on the range there was nothing to spend his earnings on so Boss, on one of the trips into town, introduced him to his bank manager and Jerry started his own account.

Boss knew his business which was mainly wool. Wool which was in high demand, and Boss's careful husbandry ensured that his was of the finest quality and took the best money at auction. The ranch thrived - and so did Jerry. Now tall and strong he needed few instructions to get the work done often pre-empting Boss's next requirement. In a word he became an essential part of the business.

Boss's wife Ruth liked him and treated him as one of the family, whilst the daughters soon got fed-up with trying to tease him and left him be - for the moment that is.

***

The eldest girl, Juney, was just eighteen when there was a subtle but noticeable change on the ranch. Boss and Ruth had not taken a long holiday for some years. The ranch had made them a small fortune and they were becoming determined to make some use of it. Boss was considering a change. All of which was suddenly brought to a head in a most unusual and for Jerry a painful manner.

As with many a teenage lass, Juney had formed a crush on the now tall, strong, and handsome Jerry. She knew all about the reproductive system from observations about the ranch, and had decided to try it out for herself. On one very hot day a scantily dressed Juney using the excuse that she wanted help to find a shoe she said she had lost, enticed Jerry into the barn making it plain as she lay back on a pile of wool just what it was she wanted. She was so incensed at Jerry's cursory rejection that she ran from the barn with her clothing in disarray screaming that Jerry had forced himself on her. As it happened Boss was in town so it was left to Ruth to console Juney and ask Jerry to retire until Boss got back to deal with it.

Boss on his return heard all Juney had to say, called on Jerry and merely said to a very shaken lad that they would talk in the morning. Jerry feared the worst, and found sleep hard to come by.

Dawn broke, and a very nervous Jerry made himself ready to face Boss. He had a deep sense that things were about to change. However he could never have imagined what was about to happen.

Even before breakfast Boss was waiting for him and without a word waved him into the room he called `the study' - the only room with any books in it where Boss did his `accounts', and partook of an occasional large nip of scotch. Boss eased himself into the big chair behind the desk and nodded for Jerry to take the other opposite.

Boss picked up a pencil and began to play with it whilst still saying nothing.

Jerry thought that he had never seen Boss look more serious, and began to fear the worst.

Boss seemed suddenly to make up his mind and looking at the pencil he was twiddling he began -

`Now lad, what's all this with you and my daughter?'

`I did absolutely nothing Boss, that's the God honest truth,' Jerry replied.

Boss raised his eyes and gazed at Jerry for some time as if trying to assess if he was lying or telling the truth. Then he slowly allowed a barely perceptive smile to reach his lips which very gradually turned into a grin.

`Well lad, I'm not going to ask if you did what Juney says because I know you and I know my girl, but she's a good looking lass and you could have been tempted - but I know you would never risk what you have here just for a few moments of illicit pleasure - and the girl has made up stories before. So you're in the clear.' Here he stopped for a long moment studying Jerry's reaction. Then as if in some way he was satisfied by what he saw he continued -

`But the thing has happened and the situation here is now difficult, as I'm sure you realise.'

Suddenly Boss seemed to be annoyed by the pencil and threw it down with some force, he sat up straight shrugged and then leaned forward eagerly.

`I've been givin' a bit of brain power to your future, lad; and although I don't want to lose you I think it's about time you stood on your own feet,' he said.

Hell's teeth he's giving me the sack, and I've done nothing. Boss read the disappointment in the lads face, and suddenly grinned.

`So I have a proposition for you.'

Now what! Thought Jerry, but could never in his wildest dreams have guessed what was about to be presented to him.

Boss took a breath, then- `The government is offering tracts of land in the Northern Territories up for sale at give away prices. Now I know you have money saved and I can guess how much. I am prepared to match that dollar for dollar to buy one of these plots. You can consider it as a gift for the years of hard work you've put in for me. And we're overstocked here so I will provide you with a good few beasts to start you off. And you will need help to build some accommodation. What do you think lad - it would be a good start for you?'

Jerry was floored, the idea of being his own boss took his breath away. His own place - a dream. He was taken aback by

Boss's generous offer, but he reckoned that he had no choice anyway.

Boss broke in, `So - from then on it will be up to you. But you've nothing more to learn from me. So what do you say, eh?'

At first Jerry could say nothing, his thoughts were in turmoil.

`Er............ thank you,' Jerry managed. `it sounds great, er... damn it I don't know how to thank you. You saved my life and now this.... Thank you.' Then after a moments thought, `but what about you and this place?' He asked.

`Don't worry lad, the girls `ll miss you and so will I, they'll just have to muck in,' he laughed. `They'll maybe think twice before throwing themselves at the nearest bloke. Beggin' yer pardon lad.'

Boss had his answer as the lad's serious expression was slowly replaced by a wide grin, and then he laughed out loud. The deal was on.

`Hells damned teeth,' was all he could say. And he held out his hand and they shook and grinned broadly at each other, now as man to man.

***

Of the available plots they successfully negotiated for a good piece of the Territory, not quite as good as Boss's place but fertile enough, and with possibilities of improvement. An important aspect was its situation straddling a good clean creek, a tributary of the river Ord which had its source high in the Kimberly range of mountains. It was a water course that was to eventually seriously impact Jerry's life.

Hiring a couple of hands from the local `town' Boss and Jerry set about building the house and some of the much needed barns and out buildings for sheering and stores. They were ready in a surprisingly short time, and the first sheep were rounded up and amidst much noise and dust loaded into carts, driven over, and were soon settled in. Boss even presented him with one of his good dogs, she was with pup and the ranch was immediately full of farm noise.

Jerry couldn't believe his luck, shook Boss's hand and thanked him again for the thousandth time.

`Yer'll be all right lad, I reckon, it looks chucka to me. And remember - any problems get hold of me. And by the way I still owe you thanks for all the stuff you did back there. Just keep in touch, I know it's a fair distance but you won't get lost.' And with that he was gone.

During the building Jerry had the opportunity to meet his neighbours and liked what he saw. They, like him, were starting out on their own and were prepared to muck-in and lend a hand whenever they could. They were a sparse little group spread over a huge area and mostly only met in the local bar when on a shopping expedition. The `town' boasted a rather seedy hotel with its attendant bar, a barber's shop, and a store that sold everything from petrol to bandages, and from furniture to farming equipment, oh yes and food. If it wasn't there Big Sid could probably get it within a day or two. For anything else it meant a longish trip to the `Main Place' with its big store, its church and its school.

The only potential trouble came in the shape of the native population some of whom bitterly resented the ruthless stealing of land they had lived on since ancestral times. Jerry however was befriended by a youngish couple whom he took in as hired help in exchange for food, accommodation and occasional cash handouts. They proved to be loyal and hard working, although they would go walk-about now and then without warning, they did however only do this when work was slack.

His first year established Jeremiah in `Good Luck Farm' and he did very well to break even. This was most encouraging, assuring him of a good sized profit in his second year. Work on the ranch took all of Jerry's available time and to look after the domestic side of life he was fortunate to be able to take on a girl of about his own age, a near neighbour as a daily help. Now Mary McDuff, the daughter of a wealthy Scottish mining engineer, Archie, had been well educated at a boarding school in Sydney and thus far she had no clear idea as to what to do with her life. So the task of looking after Jerry was a welcome one, especially as there was no suitable alternative locally. It just so happened that she was also by any standards a very good looking lass. Long dark hair with shades of red in certain lighting framed a naturally happy face and bounced invitingly on her slender shoulders. Shortish, with a trim but noticeably feminine figure, she was nevertheless tough enough to cope with the work around the house, and even help on the land when required. She was in a word just what Jerry needed.

It was only a matter of time before Jerry found himself nervously approaching the McDuff's place to ask for permission to marry Mary. The answer was a foregone conclusion as Archie had been waiting for this for some time. The pair were obviously well suited, and he liked and admired Jerry for his tenacity and his resilient approach to difficulties.

`Yes,' he thought, `she'll do well with him,' and reverently wished Mary's mother was still alive to see it.

So in the third year on the ranch they were married at the McDuff's place by the visiting parson and registrar. It was quite a `do' with McDuffs from as far way as Sydney. Jerry was delighted that Boss and his wife were able to make it. And twelve months later their daughter Matilda was born, big and healthy.

Jeremiah could now, for the first time since moving in, afford to indulge himself in a little free time. There had always been talk of people finding precious stones in the creeks here about, but no-one would divulge who these fortunates were. and Jerry put it down to wishful thinking. But it did not stop him paddling about in his creek just in case. It was on one such break from the farm toil when Jerry was sitting on the bank that he spotted, in a shallow back-water, a small group of small grey stone whose colour caused them stand out from the rest of the stony stream bed. He paddled in and carefully lifted them out for closer inspection. Had he stumbled on a rich find or were they just plain stones - he didn't know. He wrapped them in his handkerchief and returned them to his pocket. As luck would have it on his return he found a panic in place - several sheep had escaped through a gap created when the fence gave way where the stock were want to rub themselves. On his way out to sort matters he merely tipped the stones into an empty saucer on the shelf in one of the outhouses and forgot about them. And there they lay like a time bomb waiting to go off, and when it did it would change their lives for ever.

Matilda grew into a fine strapping lass, the sort that most of the young land owners for miles around saw as a very suitable wife. Courted by George Tillsley the son of the town's merchant she was soon married and as the ranch had grown considerably meantime the pair moved in, and Matilda made Jerry a proud grand-parent with a daughter of her own.

It was when Lilly was only four when she unwittingly lit the fuse.

The little girl was always free to go anywhere she chose as long as she stayed within earshot of any one of the adults, but not having either brothers or sisters she was often bored and would take to exploring the hidden corners of the ranch. It was on one such occasion that poking around one of the sheds she found the saucer in which nestled the little grey stones left there by Jerry half a lifetime ago and forgotten. She took them outside and seeing some old disused guttering leaning against the wall she took these one at a time and using straw bails to rest them on, and setting them end to end, she made a neat run to roll the stones down. So here she was about to become the catalyst to change.

As the little girl sat in the sun happily rolling these little stones down the gently sloping gutter, one of Jerry's neighbours having some business with him and was trying to find him when he stumbled on young Lilly and stopped to watch the girl playing. Simply fascinated at first with what the child had made he bent down and began to play with the stones himself. Suddenly something in his mind clicked on. Whilst handling the stones he began to wonder about them. Then he could no longer help himself, greed took over. Diverting the child's attention he managed to pocket three of the stones. Lilly did not notice and continued to play quite happily with the rest. The neighbour, Sam Tenpick, did his business with Jerry and left without disclosing his theft.

Sam, as soon as he could, visited the assay office in the Main Place, with the stones from Jerry's ranch tightly wrapped in his pocket. He thought he knew a thing or two about a thing or two and judged the stones to be worth plenty, if they were he would get his friends together to buy Jerry out, and they would be rich.

On entering the office he first asked the man to close and lock the door.

`Oh dear it's one of those,' the assayist thought, but did as he was bid.

`I would like to value these,' said Sam, tipping the three stones onto the bench.

The assay man picked up each of the stones in turn, gazed at them through his eye magnifier and weighed them. He took his time trying to think how to deal with the situation. If Sam thought he knew a bit, the assay man new considerably more. He knew his stuff and had been there a very long time. He made up his mind.

`It will cost you one hundred dollars per stone for the information,' he declared.

`Bloody hell!' Said Sam taken aback.

`Take it or leave it,' said the assayist.

The good man had seen stones exactly like these before and he knew they were stolen and he knew they were from the stream on Jeremiah's ranch. And he knew much more but would not tell Sam any of this, but he would tell Jerry all he knew.

Greed drove Sam. `I'll need to go to the bank to get the cash, and I will be back.' He pocketed the stones and charged through the door held open by the assay man.

Back in the office, the assay man told the truth. `You've a good find there, each of those stones properly cut will be worth at least four times what you have just paid me for this information. If you can find more you could be rich.' This last bit was the sting in the tail.

Sam grinned, 'I sure will be back with plenty,' said a now confident and very excited Sam. 'I want your word you will tell no one of this,' he added.

'You have my word I will not mention your visit to anyone,' promised the assay man.

And Sam left to put his plan into action.

Closing the door after him, the assayist smiled to himself and prepared to visit 'Good Luck Farm'. He would go after dark - it was imperative that he keep his trip secret.

What he had to tell Jerry would fill that man with anger at the duplicity of his trusted neighbour, and then with an ice cold determination to make the most out of the situation which both men knew was about to take place. Jerry thanked the assay man and told him that he would reimburse him for his trouble, but the good man only wanted to see justice done, as in due course it surely would.

While Sam was getting his cronies together, Jerry was weighing up the situation at the ranch. He had for some time been considering his own future and that of his family. He was feeling that he would like to own one of those big houses in Sydney and maybe do a bit of fishing or even sailing before he was too old and he knew Mary felt the same. In addition it was clear that young George had little interest in farming - he wanted to take up engineering, and a college in Sydney would do just nicely. So Jerry held a family meeting and without telling what he knew, he found that they were behind him - if they had a decent offer for the place he would sell and they would move to Sydney.

And all they had to do was to wait.

And they did not have to wait for long.

It was a stinking hot day when a sweaty and nervous Sam Tenpick arrived at the ranch to find a cool and relaxed Jerry sitting in the shade of the barn sipping from a full glass of beer. Sam checked - no one else was about.

`Murderous hot,' said Sam eyeing the beer.

`Sure is,' replied Jerry, `sorry about the beer - it's the last one. Must go into town tomorrow.'

Sam sat on a bail, and looked around him.

`You planning to stay here for ever?' Sam said conversationally.

`Well just until I've finished this drink,' Jerry said, deliberately misunderstanding.

Sam forced a laugh.

Jerry waited.

Sam bit the bullet, and leaning back said slowly - `It's a good place this, probably worth a good bit as a going concern, what with the stock and all that, eh?'

Jerry sipped his beer appreciatively, and waited.

`A couple of the lads and me were discussing what was going to happen to this place if you were to retire, eh?'

Jerry waited.

A hot and frustrated Sam jumped in with both feet.

`We thought we might make you an offer for the spread, as a working farm of course,' he added as an after thought.

Jerry took another sip of beer, and waited.

`We thought about.' Sam mentioned a figure which was about what Jerry reckoned the place as worth, `would be about right?'

Jerry swallowed the last of his drink. `Well I'd better be getting back to work,' he said.

WITCHCRAFT and other fateful tales

A long and awkward silence followed. Both men knew it couldn't end there.

Sam broke first.

`Well what do you say?' he asked bluntly. This time they were doing the deal.

Jerry laughed. `Remember this is all I have to retire on,' he failed to mention a nice nest egg in the bank. `I could not consider anything less than,' and he stated a sum that was four times that which Sam had offered. He knew Sam and knew his greed.

But Sam was genuinely appalled. Jerry's price was by any standards ridiculously too high.

`You can't be serious.' Was all he could find to say.

`Take it or leave it,' said Jerry standing up to indicate that the discussion was at an end. `Work,' he said waving his glass towards the inside of the barn.

Jerry watched Sam's retreating back, shirt stained dark with perspiration, and knew he'd be back.

***

Jerry eventually settled for a figure that was three times what Sam had originally offered and was three times what the place was worth. And Jerry had also rescued the remaining stones from where Lilly with promises of the toy of her dreams said she had hidden them. They proved to be worth a great deal in themselves.

So a very wealthy Jeremiah Saul and his family moved to Sydney where Jerry bought the house of his dreams, and did a lot of fishing and a little sailing. They exchanged visits with Boss, now an elderly man but still able to get about.

`I knew you'd do well young Jerry,' he said `even as I pulled you out of the drink' and they laughed uproariously.

The news of the diamond find on Jerry's ranch reached the nationals and there was much flinging about of money as prospectors fought for the privilege of owning land supposedly cascading with diamonds. The run was short lived as strangely only a few very poor quality gems were ever found. Although later a fortune of diamonds was and still is mined in the Kimberly hills far above Good Luck Farm.

What the assay man told Jerry but failed to mention to Sam was that the stones he brought to have valued were identical to ones he had seen before and his geologist adviser and friend had studied them and the terrain in which they had been found. What he discovered was that they were left over from a great storm which took place on the Kimberlies about one hundred years previously and the flood waters had carried any and all loose diamonds away down stream far onto the plains and were essentially lost. It was possible, he had said, that there may be the odd corner in some remote stream where one or two had remained stuck. Such were the ones Sam brought in.

The farm was resold as a ranch and Sam died a year later - he was broke.

JML
21/12/2008

ENCHANTMENT

*I*t came upon him as a shock. After all, at the ripe old age of thirty he reckoned that he had had more than his fair share of adventures with members of the opposite gender. Most had by now faded into the anonymity of time, but just a couple were still held crisp and clear in his memory causing his heart to beat faster, and his face to break into a smile when he brought them to mind. But this - this was very, very different.

To begin with Terry Childes was not particularly attractive in the conventional sense. A mere five foot eight or so, nevertheless every inch of her was charged with a vivid energy that radiated out from her person and lit her surroundings wherever she was.

She was impossible to ignore, and she could take her choice from any of the many men who tried to impress her.

So why did she choose him? The answer to that question came too late to save him.

And choose him she did, deliberately, and with care; but to begin with she led him to believe that he made all the running.

Charles Henry Worth rejoiced as being well advanced in his profession, he was a fully trained and qualified value assessor of residential buildings and their contents.

Highly thought of by the well respected firm for whom he worked, he was sent all over the British Isles putting a value on goods and chattels left by the deceased, mostly of the very wealthy. It had taken many years to establish his reputation and it had paid well as demonstrated by the size of his own house and the quality of the fast car he flashed around in.

Apart from the high value assets he surrounded himself with you would not give Charles a second look. Ordinary was one's overall impression, even plain - with the exception of a mop of bright red hair, a gift from his father whom he closely resembled in life. His Mother had outlived her spouse by only a year leaving Charles to fend for himself, which with characteristic ease he solved by employing a daily housekeeper and a gardener. The one thing which breathed excitement into this rather dull individual was films. An active member of two film societies, Charles would travel the length and breadth of the country just to see a single showing of some rare old movie.

However it was at his local film club that he first noticed Terry. Such was the instant impression she created that he immediately thought he had seen her somewhere before.

Serious green-grey eyes casually appraised him. Eyes whose brightness was enhanced by the contrasting dark brown hair that curled naturally to frame her face. Later he would notice her perfect nose and lips that seemed to breath passion. Her figure when she moved into full view was the kind that no full blooded male would not appreciate - the word that sprung to Charles's mind was simply - gorgeous. If you were any normal man you would certainly not miss our Terry.

Before Charles could think what to do, the film under discussion was announced and everyone took a seat, the lights were dimmed and the show began. After the film, when the lighting was restored, Terry was nowhere to be seen. Disappointingly from Charles's point of view she had not stayed for the discussion which normally followed such showings. He would like to have heard her opinion of the film. It was then during the discussion that he realised that Terry had made such an impression on him that he found it hard to recollect enough of the plot to make a single intelligent comment, let alone any comprehensive assessment, which for him was unusual. Always keen to demonstrate his wide knowledge of the cinema it had become routine for him to give the members the benefit of his views, which to be fair were usually worth listening to.

She was not at the next several meetings of either society. He did look, and felt a sense of loss when she did not make an appearance, but the quality of the films absorbed his mind and he forgot about her - or almost.

Then there she was again. He tried to sit next to her, but was beaten to it by a handsome athletic individual who seemed to be on intimate terms with her. That feeling of disappointment again. With an effort he concentrated on the film which fortunately was an important one in the history of cinema and one of which he knew something. It was therefore easy for him to stand up after the film and give the assembled members the benefit of his knowledge. The members showed their appreciation and as they were breaking up to leave several crowded round him to continue the discussion informally. It was during this interchange that he felt a tug on his sleeve, and there she was smiling at him only inches away.

`Thank you,' she said, `I very much liked what you said about the film.' But by the time this had registered in his mind she was gone with a wave of her hand. Afterwards all he could remember was how easy on the ear her voice was.

And she again vanished for several meetings. He tentatively asked about her of a couple of members, but whilst they recognised her from his description they had no idea who she was. One of them said she was comparatively new to the group.

Then a surprise.

Charles had on occasion purchased the odd rare copy of an old film on the Inter-net. He was browsing looking for some such opportunity when there it was - one of those for which he had long been searching. The name was simply `Terry' and there was an Inter-net address. He naturally assumed Terry was male and so he suggested an evening meeting at a local pub with a view to his making a purchase assuming the quality of the film was satisfactory. It was agreed that they would each make for the window table at seven on the next evening.

As he entered and saw who was already seated at that particular table, Charles hesitated. But spotting him the girl waved him over.

`Hallo Charles,' she said, `I'm Terry, do please sit down.'

Completely taken aback, Charles simply sat and gazed at her.

Dressed simply in a top and skirt of some slinky material, greenish grey to match her eyes exactly, she looked flawless.

Charles thought he must be dreaming, and with an effort he pulled himself together.

`I'm sorry,' he began, `but I had no idea it was you.' It was all he could think of to say.

She prompted him - `Would you please get me a drink?'

`Of course, what would you like?'

`A dry red wine please - a large one if you don't mind?'

He had to ask, after returning with the drinks, `The message on the net said that you had a film for sale - a quite rare one?'

Terry giggled at this. `I'm awfully sorry,' she said, `I just didn't know how to get you on your own, do you mind?'

`No of course not,' he replied smiling broadly.

And so began an evening and a relationship that was bring his freedom to an end.

***

At first it was all about films. They met at the club and began to have meals out together, most often at lunch time but on occasion in the evening. Terry mesmerised him, Charles became totally besotted, but despite his crude attempts to entertain her at home, she always seemed to have an excuse.

Strangely, she seemed to know quite a bit about Charles's history. She knew where he worked and what his work entailed. How she knew he never found out. He was considerably flattered that she showed a keen interest in his work, and was only too happy to tell her of all the fascinating places and objects he was required to place a value on, just so that greedy relatives could fight over them. But in spite of his many questions she remained a complete mystery, her past an unknown. Charles did not even know where she lived. But her secrecy did not unduly trouble him as when she kissed him she seemed to promise him everything. And he lived for those kisses, and those sweet and tender moments she occasionally allowed him. He wanted her badly and she let him believe that she would one day be his, and this promise dragged him deeper in.

Then one day just after Christmas she gave in and led him to believe that she would move in with him by the following Christmas. Charles was over the moon, his eyes were so full of Terry they could see nothing else. It was like one of those movies they were so keen on. The projector was whirring, and the images on the screen were flickering through the action - But this was real life and Charles could no longer tell the difference.

Terry was like quick silver, he would seem to have her - when she would suddenly vanish from the scene, and no-one knew where she was. She would turn up after several days saying with a beauteous smile 'My aunt was ill.' or some such thing, and giving him a kiss it would then be all right again.

Then one evening, when she allowed him to take her to his home, she began to talk about money. She had had a windfall from a distant relative who had passed on. 'And I don't want to pay tax on it, could I use your account for a while? After all it will be both our account one day?' She smiled and kissed him, and he arranged for her to have access to it. And he would see no problem with this. His critical faculties had deserted him, and this movie still had some time to run.

Then Terry started missing appointments with Charles often after arranging to meet in the strangest of places.

The answer to Charles's puzzled questions was as always to put her arms round him lifting her face for that inevitable kiss. Poor Charles! If only he had someone with whom to share his growing anxieties. The euphoria that drove their earlier relationship with its promises of love fulfilled had begun to change ever so slowly. A feeling of lack of progress was beginning to eat into Charles's anticipation. This feeling of his future with Terry slipping away grew when she was missing, only to be reduced to renewed passion when she returned.

The Christmas of promise approached and Charles's eagerness grew with every day that passed. He was riding high with anticipation when it happened.

The morning was normal, he was due for a ten a.m. meeting at the local office and he was taking his time over breakfast, when the door chimes interrupted his thoughts. On opening the door he was surprised to see not one but three policemen standing there.

Before he had a chance to ask the obvious question, one of them, a sergeant, spoke.

`Mr Charles Worth?' He asked.

`Yes,' Charles replied.

`I'm sorry sir, but we are making some general enquiries about a number of break-ins to some local places, may we come in?' This last was a statement rather than a question. Charles showed them into the living room where the sergeant suggested that they all be seated.

Charles had no idea of what was to come and merely sat and politely waited for them to begin.

`I am Sergeant Smithers and these are PC Allen and PC Twellis,

`I understand that you are employed as a valuer by Jenkins and Son, and that you have recently visited,' and here he mentioned three large houses, `in order to value buildings and contents?' Again this was a statement not a question.

`That's correct,' replied Charles, `how can I help?'

The sergeant apologised again, and said, `I'm afraid that we have had a tip off that you may have taken items which do not belong to you, and we have obtained a warrant to search this premises.' And without waiting for Charles's reaction he nodded to the two PCs who immediately stood and began opening drawers.

The process took just less than an hour after which they returned to the living room, and pulled their chairs round to face him. One of them produced a notebook and pencil and the sergeant began by placing four small black leather covered boxes on the table and opened them to reveal four magnificent items of jewellery which sparkled in the rays of the morning sun as it spilled into the room.

'Do these belong to you sir?' The sergeant asked.

Charles was out of his depth, what the hell was going on, he recognised these items instantly. He had only recently been paid handsomely to place a value on each of them as part of an assessment of three separate properties. But he had no idea how they came to be here. He began to suspect a police plant - but why pick on him?

The sergeant was patient.

'I'll ask you again sir. Do these items belong to you sir?'

Poor Charles, he had no choice.

'Er................no,' he said finally. 'But.....'

He got no further, the sergeant interrupted him -

'Then I have no choice sir, but to ask you to accompany us to the station for questioning. We also need copies of your bank statements covering the last twelve months or so. And you might need any aid memoir as to your movements over say the same period.' And in reply to Charles's question -'No sir you are not under arrest we just want answers to a few questions, like where were you at certain times.'

***

At the station they took his finger prints and a DNA sample - 'To eliminate you from the enquiry. - Just a formality sir.'

'Of course you will find my prints on the boxes, and my DNA - I valued these items myself and the assistant who is always also present at the evaluation will verify that these things were still there when we left the premises - and I assure you that I have not been back since.' Charles began to realise the seriousness of his position and insisted in having a lawyer present before they went any further.

Jenkins and Sons, certain of his integrity did not hesitate to provide the company's solicitor, Mr Young, at his disposal.

However things for Charles began to look black when they found out that he had no good explanation for his whereabouts between eight pm and midnight on the days when the break-ins had taken place. Checking with his diary these where the times when Terry had agreed to meet him at some strange out of town venue, and had not turned up.

In addition the police produced a woman who had seen him 'lurking suspiciously' at one of these places on the day of the break-in. 'A man with red hair,' she said, and picked him out of an identification parade. Worse - they found a taxi driver who knew him and had been hired by Charles to drop him off at another of the places and also on the very night of that break-in.

Then there was the bank account. He had no explanation for the four deposits of several thousand pounds each and a very recent withdrawal of one hundred thousand pounds which left him almost broke.

In this film the baddies were winning - this was not in the script.

The police felt they had a good case and charged Charles with the break-ins, and of stealing at least twenty-five items of very valuable jewellery, and of handling stolen goods. They thought he would get at least five years.

Charles was considered not to be a threat to public safety, and was released on bail. A date for his trial was set.

***

A desperate Charles tried in every way he knew to find Terry, but failed completely. Several male members of both film clubs remembered her but had no idea how to get hold of her or where she might be. The Inter-net address which had started the whole thing off was discontinued.

She had gone - simply gone.

Seven short days to go, and a miserable Charles was nursing a drink in front of his lounge fire, musing over his naivety when the door chimes claimed his attention. He opened the door.

And there on his very doorstep stood Terry, with that smile.

`May I come in?' She said.

Charles merely stood aside, and she brushed past him.

Sat on each side of the fire, she asked for and received a drink. Charles again said nothing, and waited. He thought she looked more beautiful than ever.

Her green-grey eyes looked thoughtful.

`As you may have guessed I am now considerably wealthy, thanks to you, and the sale of several items'

Charles merely nodded.

`Terry Childes is not my real name, and I now live abroad, so when I leave here you will never find me. I shall be gone out of your life for ever.'

Charles waited, grimfaced. This person sitting comfortably in his house drinking his sherry was the cause of all his recent trouble, and which now looked destined to deprive him of his freedom. Was she here just to gloat?

`Don't worry,' she continued, and patted a large envelope which she had place on the arm of her chair, `I have here a full confession with dates and times and other evidence that will convince the police of your complete innocence. It is a sworn statement and has been formally notarised. It does however not yet have my proper signature.'

She grinned and sipped her drink appreciatively.

`Exactly twenty-four hours from now the original with my signature will be delivered to the police by special courier. In the meantime I will leave you with this.' She again patted the envelope.

There was a longish pause.

`Why me?' Said Charles.

`I did my research,' she replied, `and you were just perfect.'

She swallowed the rest of her drink and stood.

`Well this really is goodbye,' she said with a certain sadness in her voice.

At the door she turned to him and said -

`By the way the whole idea for all of this came from one of those old films you showed at the film club.'

And she was gone.

JML
26/12/2008

ROOM 423

He peered cautiously round a corner of the corridor, and as he did so his hand went to his inside pocket and his fingers felt the familiar comfort of his neat Italian automatic with its silencer. As he leaned cautiously out he wondered if he would hear the next shot aimed at him, or whether his brains would make a piece of modern graffiti on the nearby wall. He wondered if he had been followed, he had done his best to shake off any such a threat - but he couldn't be sure - they were good, damned good. In answer to his thought a bullet slammed into the door jamb inches from his ear, and almost immediately came the short chilling sound made by a silencer. He felt cornered. The lift was nearer to his would-be killer but the fire exit stairs were closer to him. Drawing his automatic he readied himself, then all in one movement he fired a couple of shots along the corridor, hoping as he did that there were no innocent parties in the way, and ran for the stairs.

As he clattered down the bare steps as fast as he could, he heard curses from above followed by a couple more puffs from a silencer and the whine of deflected bullets. At the bottom a bang on the door release bar and he tumbled out onto a crowded pavement crammed with shoppers and end of day business men. Safe. For the moment.

He hailed a taxi without any clear idea what answer to give the driver in reply to his obvious question. Not home, it would be watched. He could do with a drink .

`Just drop me off at a decent pub, but make it at least a couple of miles from here,' he said. Not an unusual kind of request for this driver, he had seen them all in his time.

The pub was a good choice, not too busy and not too quiet. He ordered a pint of bitter and chose a seat with its back to the wall and a good view of the door. He began to relax.

What he had found in the flat he had so recently vacated needed some considerable thought. Used as he was to the sight of serious crime this one was a puzzle. Nothing about it was familiar. Even how he came to be there was mind bogglingly weird.

- An unfamiliar voice on his phone had interrupted a spare few minutes he had taken to get the latest TV news. All the voice said was the address, and finished with - `Take your weapon, and don't be followed.' So this he had done and nearly at the expense of his life.

He was desperate for answers, and so far he had none. He did not even know the right questions to ask.

But first, he needed a safe place to rest his head.

He thumbed his phone.

`Yes, OK love,' said Maisie, `just this once. But I want no trouble mind, and you sleep on the couch.'

More relaxed now after a second pint, he took a cab to Maisie's.

In answer to his pressing the bell the door opened just as far as the chain would allow, and from the internal gloom Maisie's voice called out an unwelcoming -`Yes, who is it, and what do you want?'

`It's me, love. Can I come in?' He answered.

The chain rattled and the door opened just a wee bit more as Maisie took a look. Then there she was, her expression a mixture of question and pleasure. They had once been lovers. The thing had not lasted long but they had parted good friends.

`Well don't stand there like a wet flannel, move your stumps and come on in.'

He did as he was bid and followed her into the familiar warmth of the cosy sitting room. As he sat on the settee Maisie poured him a whiskey from the collection of bottles and glasses she always had ready, and without a word carried it across to him, she then picked up her own unfinished gin, and waved it at him. `Cheers,' she said.

`Likewise,' he said, `and thanks.'

They sat smiling at each other for a while, whilst sipping their drinks. Maisie knew better than to ask him awkward questions. He was there and in need, and for the moment that was enough. His business and his movements had always been a mystery to her, and they both wanted to keep it that way. For him Maisie's was his safe haven. Here he could relax and take time to think, and he desperately needed to think, he felt that his survival depended on his next move.

`When did you last eat?' Maisie asked eventually. `Not for some time I bet?' And without waiting for reply she bustled off to busy herself in the kitchen. As the sounds of domestic activity reached him through the open door, he began to think.

First, it was clear that he hadn't a clue as to what he seemed to be involved in. Scuttling about with a loaded automatic and being shot at was not part of his normally peaceful life style. Just what the hell was happening? The facts were plain enough, but they did not make any kind of sense. He had no idea who it was who phoned him to direct him to the flat. The voice was not familiar.

The flat had been a shock. He had found the door ajar, its lock smashed. Inside was a mess with broken furniture lying everywhere and documents were scattered about. But it was the spare room clearly used as a small office that brought him to an abrupt halt. Every surface, floor walls and ceiling was liberally splashed with what he took to be blood. But whose it was or who had caused it to be there - there was no sign.

Feeling sick he turned to leave and as he did so he noticed the corner of an envelope lit by a random beam from the evening sun. He picked it up and found to his astonishment that it had his name on it, typed in bold letters and mysteriously free from even the smallest trace of blood.

It was as he pocketed the envelope and made his way to the door that he heard the unmistakable click, click of a safety catch being thumbed off - a hand gun being made ready to fire.

Much later, relaxing in Maisie's friendly presence he remembered the envelope, found it, and very carefully prised open the flap. Inside was a CD, and that was all.

Was this what everyone was after, even prepared to kill for? If so what the hell was on it?

Just then Maise re-entered with two steaming bowls of home made soup, chunks of fresh bread and eating implements. The CD could wait.

After they had eaten they sat reminiscing in the way that familiar friends do, and as it got dark Maisie kissed him lightly `Good night love, tomorrow will be better,' she promised, and went to bed, leaving him with blanket and pillow.

Once on his own he turned the TV sound down and slotted the CD into the player on the assumption that it might be a DVD. The screen remained blank. The disk must contain digital data he thought and replaced it in the envelope. He would need access to a computer to determine its contents - that would have to be tomorrow.

**

Waking he found that Maisie had left for work, she was a waitress in a busy city café where she was well paid as an attraction, which she was. His breakfast was on the table. He ate. Washed up. Propped a note to Maisy against a jug telling her he would be back come evening. Phoned a cab and left. In the cab he phoned George. George was a wiz with any kind of electronics, and computers were his bread and butter. If you had a computer problem George could be relied on to fix it; for a price.

An unkempt George let him in. George was not one to waste time in tidying either himself or his place and they weaved their way through piles of books and magazines and entered the big dining room which was totally given over to computers, printers and other associated hardware. `Mind the wires,' George warned unnecessarily.

`Break just one connection and it might take me days to find it.'

He looked at the disordered tangle and placed his feet with care.

`Tea?' George asked. `You can tell me what your problem is while we sup.'

George vanished into the kitchen leaving him to find a free space in which to sit.

He was grateful for the drink, which they finished in silence. George knew him well enough not to press him, he would come clean in his own time.

'Right,' he said, discarding his cup, 'I am unsure about involving you in this thing, it could be very dangerous. I have already been shot at. Also I have no idea what it is all about.' He paused to let this warning sink in. 'But there is no-one I can trust other than you, but I'll understand if you don't want to know.'

George gazed at him over his cup concealing a broad grin.

'That's OK,' he said, 'life's just got interesting. So what 've you got that needs me?'

He smiled at George, thanks could come later.

'What I have here is a disk,' he waved it, 'and I require to know what is on it.'

George held his hand out for the item, removed it carefully from its envelope and looked at it, turning it over several times.

'Can you do it?' He asked.

'Depends on several factors,' replied George, and continued to study the disk. But it told him nothing. 'Do you want to leave it with me, it could take a while?'

'No I'll stay if you don't mind, I've nothing better to do.' and he settled down in his chair.

George disappeared into the inner sanctum which shared its space with more electronic gear and technical literature stacked on shelves and lying on every level surface. In spite of his warning that it might take some time, George returned to a snoring visitor in just about half an hour.

He awoke with a start and took a minute or so to work out where he was, and realization slowly dawned as he gazed at George's puzzled face. `Well?' He asked.

George waved the disk about. `The format is bog standard, and the data is unprotected so it was easy, anyone with a standard pc could find out what is on it. Not much. I have searched the whole disk and all I can find is a few numbers which mean nothing to me.'

For some reason he found this disappointing, he was hoping to find a message which would explain his involvement in whatever this was.

George handed him a small piece of paper on which he had written the numbers -

"22 - 32 - 12
12/3"

Having read what was written he looked up at George and asked, `Well what does it mean?'

George shrugged, `You've got me there laddie, I have no idea.'

`Think,' he said, `it must mean something.' An obvious statement if ever there was one.

They tried everything, from map references to foreign telephone numbers, and even e-mail addresses - but nothing fitted. All day they tried, until it became obvious to both that they would not succeed that day, and agreed to part and keep in contact should either of them find a solution.

George stood at his door and watched him dive into the cab he had ordered and returned indoors to continue to find an answer. He felt that they had given it their best shot and that they were doomed never to work it out.

It was left to a coincidence that he stumbled on the answer, or at least a part of it. It had got to evening and he called at the off-licence near to Maisie's. It was only a small local shop and was not yet blessed with the card payment machinery, one had to pay with cash or by some other means. In his case he knew the owner well enough from frequent visits to top up Maisie's reserves to pay by cheque. It was as he was making out his cheque that he notice the bank code printed together with the bank's name on each of the blank cheque forms. It comprised three groups of two digits separated by dashes - exactly like the first row of numbers on the disk. And although the actual numbers were different they clearly referred to a bank. He still had no idea what the other numbers were but it was, he felt, a start.

Now he was getting somewhere.

He was quite light hearted as with the bag of booze in one hand he rang Maisie's bell with the other.

It was left to Maisie later that night to suggest that the second set of numbers refered to a safe deposit box held at the bank which was identified by the first set of numbers.

He was elated and swung Maisie round, until his enthusiasm was crushed by her observation that -

`Of course you will need the key.'

Key, he thought, of course, there were normally two keys for every box, one was always held by the bank whilst the other was handed to the customer. A dead end?

By morning he had a plan, or the bones of one. Fingers Frank, no one knew his surname, was an old hand at working with keys. Just the man, he thought, if he was out of prison. A cab ride later he was outside Frank's place, and asked the cabby to drive past. He was glad he did as there were a couple of heavies leaning on the wall opposite. The cab dropped him off at the rear. He scaled the fence and knocked on Frank's apology for a door.

-- Nothing!

He hammered on the wood.

This time a response.

`He aint in,' a masculine voice called out.

`That's OK, tell him that if he isn't in, I don't want to see him,' he shouted back.

Frank's grinning red face appeared at a suddenly opened window above him. `Come down you jerk, and let me in,' he called as quietly as he could.

To Frank the problem of the key was just routine.

And as the two sat on boxes, Frank began to explain.

He must ask to look in the box number 12/3, whilst a waving similar key and insist on opening the box in private. When on his own and whilst making box opening and closing noises, he must take a plasticine mold of the bank's key by pressing it into the stuff. `You bring it back here and in half an hour I'll have your key ready for use,' Frank promised.

As he left Frank's place the two toughies were still lounging about in the street trying to disguise themselves as lamp posts, but it was a con. He thought he was clear when he was felled by a blow to the head.

***

As he came round he became conscious of the pain in his head where the blow had struck, and he had no idea where he was. It was dark and he was out in the country, and amongst trees -- a wood? He must have been there some time, he was stiff and very cold. What had he been doing, it was hard to remember.

Panic ----- the paper with the deposit box number had gone - also his gun. The bastards must have taken them.

He then remembered that whoever took the paper would be unable to gain anything useful from it, as the real number had, at George's suggestion, been surrounded by other similar but meaningless numbers written in the same colour ink. Only he and George knew the real number by it's remembered position on the paper. But he would miss his gun.

Why had they left him? He wondered.

Pulling himself together he stumbled towards where he thought he could hear traffic, and quite suddenly burst out onto a very busy trunk road.

He tried to thumb a lift but no one stopped, but he did find a phone box, dialled Maisie who thankfully was in. he read the name of the booth out to her with a request that she took her car and collected him. And he sat on the grass by the phone box to wait.

∗

Maisie collected a near corpse, Almost unconscious with pain and cold she almost missed him slumped in the grassy verge a little distance from the call box. Even with 's tender care it was well over a week before he felt well enough to go out. He felt frustrated by this lack of activity, and he was missing his own place, and his gun.

It was time to get going.

He took a cab to Frank's to find the same thugs still outside and a different man in Frank's body.

'I am sorry,' he said, 'they called.' He nodded at the street. 'I can't help you any more.'

He couldn't blame Frank. 'It's OK,' he said,'I understand - you're a good mate.'

As he left by the back Frank shook his hand and as he did so he passed him a chunk of plasticine in which was embedded a blank key.

'Good luck, my friend,' Frank said. And he meant it.

***

It took only a short time to discover the name of the bank and its branch address represented by the numbers. It was a small sub-branch in the heart of one or our larger northern cities. After much persuasion and many promises he got Maisie to lend him her small car.

The day he chose proved to be cold and bleak. A mild depression overtook him which grew worse as he travelled north. He was however jerked out of this mood when he noticed the same two cars on his tail which had joined him just after he set off, and were still there as he entered the town.

A left, two rights, and another left - yes they were following him. He was both pleased and irritated at the sight as it meant that they probably still had not solved the numbers clue, otherwise why follow him? He drove fast and lost them in a maze of narrow back streets. He parked the car, made for the main street, and almost immediately caught a bus. He was lucky, the bus stopped opposite the bank. As he walked across the road he rehearsed his lines - on no account must he raise the slightest suspicion.

As it happened there were no customers waiting and he was attended immediately by a young assistant. 'Can I help you, Sir,' she asked politely.

`Yes please,' he replied, `I want to put something of value into a safe deposit box.'

`That will require the manager, sir - I'll get him for you. Would you please step into the consultation room.' And she opened the door of a small cubicle barely big enough to house two chairs and a small table.

He sat as requested, and after the murmur of voices outside a tall, stern individual entered and took the other seat.

`I understand you require access to one of our safe boxes?' he stated. What is the number?'

`Twelve slash three,' he said simply.

`Yes,' said the man, `that is one of ours. Do you have your key?'

The man looked puzzled. `Only we don't get many people these days using the safes and I remember the person who rented it. We have to be so very careful these days - and that person was a woman.

He thought fast, a woman?

`That's correct,' he said, `that was my secretary, I was unwell at the time so she did the necessary - was that OK?'

The man looked uncertain. `Key sir, do you have it?'

Frank had made him rehearse the next bit over and over again until he was perfect.

He pulled out his wallet from which he removed the blank key, which was now doctored by indelible ink to look as if it had teeth, as he flashed the key in front of the man he dropped the wallet to which he returned the key on picking it up.

It worked.

`That's all right sir, here is the other one.'

`I would like to do the next bit in private,' he said, `if you would kindly fetch my box.' He liked the `My'.

The man was gone for a nerve racking five minutes or so.

'There you are sir, it's all yours.' And he left, locking the cubicle door behind him.

Once sure the door was closed, he fitted the genuine key into one of the locks on the box and rattled it. He then remove the key and pressed it into the plasticine just as Frank had demonstrated.

He then made more rattling noises to simulate locking the box, and pressed the bell by the door to request assistance.

He thanked the man and told him that he would be back in a couple of days to retrieve that which he had just placed in his box.

'Will it be the secretary or yourself?' The man asked politely.

'It'll be me,' he replied, 'bye for now, and thanks.'

***

Maisie's car was just as he had left it, and he was not followed on the return trip.

He was considerably relieved to be back at Frank's.

'Looks OK,' Frank said after a close inspection of the impression. 'Make yourself a cup of tea - it will be ready for you in about half an hour.'

Key safely in his pocket, and his thanks said to Frank, he took advantage of some distraction at the end of the street to escape without being detected, and took a cab back to Maisie's.

He gave up worrying what was in the safe deposit box, it had felt light enough to be empty, but there was something in it as was obvious when it was shaken.

What he had got himself involved in was still as much a mystery as ever. He did not know why, what, who or how he had got mixed up in this but It could clearly cost him his life. Under his façade of total confidence he had to confess to himself to be at a loss and somewhat frightened. Indeed fear was now his constant friend. Its presence made him careful, and he felt he needed to be very careful. But - before anything else he longed for the comfort of a gun. A gun ----- even that worried him, he knew that he would use it if he had to, it had become a way of life with him, a matter of survival.

Later, relaxing in Maisie's comforting company, he tried to forget the questions that coursed continuously through his mind. Tomorrow he would try to do nothing.

But it wasn't to be like that.

Maisie had arranged for her sister to stay for a day or two and she was anxious for him to conclude his business and to be on his way - `Not that I'm pushing you,' she said.

So the very next day found him in a cab driving slowly past that bank. It was easy to see the watchers - they were too obvious - so where were the hidden ones? He paid the cabby gave him some instructions as to how he was to be collected, and asked him to go very slowly past the bank's recessed front door, at which point the launched himself across the pavement and into the doorway. As he entered he was certain he had not been seen.

This time the same girl apologised for her boss's absence , promising to deal with him herself.

He sat for some time with the box on the table and both keys lying beside it, wondering if it wouldn't be wiser to simply leave now without opening the thing.

Then with a heavy sigh he fitted both keys in the slots and rotated each one in turn. They worked perfectly, and ever so gently he lifted the lid.

Whatever he had expected to see, it was not this.

All there was lying there at the bottom was a plain envelope.

He simply sat and stared at it for some time, puzzling, but without answers.

Eventually he reached in, removed the envelope and slid it into his inside pocket, left the keys by the box on the table. He rang for and thanked the girl on the way to the door.

He called the cab and dived into it as it was driven very slowly past.

There was no one following them, and he was soon at Maisie's place.

Once inside he used his mobile phone to arrange for a gun, an Italian automatic, to be left with ammo under a stone at the base of the northern arch which took the A*** over the river. It cost him plenty but it would give him comfort - and that precious commodity he was willing to pay for.

Although Maisie was unhappy to see him still there, she cheered up at the sight of the bottle of gin he had secured on his way.

***

Several gin and tonics later he had the necessary courage to open the envelope.

Inside was a single piece of paper on which was neatly typed a number. No guessing this time as to what it meant it was a land line telephone number. He recognised the area code as being fairly local.

He sat and stared at it for a very long time.

The gin was gone and Maisie had retired when he eventually settled down to sleep. But sleep avoided him, and it was just before dawn that he dozed off having made up his mind to ring the number.

***

Maisie had left, he had eaten the breakfast she had left, when he pulled out his mobile phone and thumbed the number from the deposit box.

Another surprise.

He was half expecting a rough voice warning him - or threatening him, but what he heard was well modulated tomes of a very well educated male.

`Hallo,' it said, `As you have rung this number we must now make arrangements to meet.'

There was a pause.

`It is imperative for your own safety and that of others that you tell no one of what you will be involved in from now on. You must believe that failure to comply with this simple request could cost you your life.' The voice eventually continued. `Tomorrow you will take a cab to - here he quoted an address in the city centre - Take the lift to room 423 on the fourth floor and be there for sixteen hundred hours exactly. It is vital that you are not followed.

Pause.

`Till then good bye, and good luck.

So there it was - whatever it was.

***

On her return Maisie wanted to know all about it, and was considerably puzzled by his obvious reticence. But he told her nothing.

Very early the next day he collected the gun from where it had been carefully hidden, removed it from the waterproof covering, checked it out, and slid it into his inside pocket modified for just such a purpose.

He then made several cab journeys to ensure there was no one on his tail, lunched well at a favourite pub, puzzled all the time about the letter, and just after three thirty made his way to the notified building.

The place was impressive. Its marble front lifted itself high into the air reaching out above most of the surroundings.

As he entered the ground floor area he slid his hand into that pocket and felt the gun's familiar shape. The area was empty but he noticed several cunningly sighted CCTV cameras. Still with his hand on the gun he pressed the lift button and entered the empty lift on its arrival. Nervously he pressed the button for the fourth floor.

The lift slowed and stopped with barely a jerk.

Its door swished open, and as it did so there was noise.

Peering round the door he saw a long carpeted corridor, and in it several people were going about their business taking no notice of him whatsoever.

He thought for some moments that he had ventured into the wrong building.

Gathering himself together he entered the corridor and made his way along looking for a number 423.

He almost missed it as the door with its number was ajar.

From inside came the murmur of voices.

He made his way cautiously in, still with his hand on the gun.

Almost immediately he was spotteed by a well dressed individual seated behind a very large desk. This man stood, walked round the desk and approached him with outstretched hand.

`Ah, our Mr Rankin, Mr Michael Rankin I think. Welcome to the team. I'm pleased to see you are bang on time, and by the way you won't be needing that.' He nodded to where his hand was still nursing his gun.

He shook he offered hand feeling a little foolish and looked around him.

There were a couple of other desks with people seated at them, they were either engaged on the phone or working on some papers.

`Grab a chair,' said the big man, `you must be wondering just what this is all about.' It was a statement.

Bewildered, he just nodded.

`Well I am not sorry we have put you through all this, but we had to be sure of you, especially since you are only recently out of prison. Oh yes we know all there is to know about you,' he added.

He simply sat, even more bewildered.

The big man began again, `My name is not important, you just call me Jock, and I am your boss from now on.'

Now this was getting ridiculous.

This is a branch of her Majesty's Secret Service, you have just been through a series of tests in which you have passed with flying colours, and whether you like it or not you have just been recruited. You are now a member of our little team, and when you've got your breath back I will introduce you to the others and to your controller who will explain just what we want you to do.'

Smiling, he continued, `you will be paid a salary and certain expenses as from today.'

He paused to let this sink in.

`You can now return to your own place - but------,' his smile was replaced by a grim scowl ---------------

`There is just one more important thing - you have no choice in this, and should you not comply ---------- well you already know too much - if you get my drift.'

JML
16/1/2009

JUST A WORD OR TWO

*S*ixteen across, "Briefly, where there's evidence someone got cracking to find food," three words with letters "two, one, and eight." Richard Seemley had been struggling with it for a considerable time. Since he retired from the Civil Service, the big crossword was his breakfast ritual. It usually took him about a week to complete just when the next one was due. The clues were of the cryptic variety which he found to be excellent mental exercise, and a pleasurable means of putting his brain in gear to start the day.

Then, three 'down' clues later, he had it - 'IN A NUTSHELL'. A good one that, he thought, and glancing at the clock decided that it was time to get the day underway. The weather was warm and for once it was dry - a good day to mow the lawns.

He set the puzzle aside, dumped the pots in the sink, donned his gardening clobber and proceeded to extract the mower.

It was teeming the next day and Richard had no pressing engagement so he relaxed with his crossword which by now only had a few awkward clues unsolved.

Just as he was about to abandon the struggle something about this particular crossword caught his eye. It was nothing

165

special, just that two of the 'across' words on the same line seemed to stand out as related to one another. These were:-

INFIDELITY # DISCOVERED

Richard chuckled, so the philandered had been found out. Of the many such crosswords he had completed he had never before noticed a sequence of words that could be linked. He wondered if the compiler had realised that there might in this case be an association.

His day proved to be a busy one with some shopping and lunch out. Back home he unpacked and put away his purchases, opened the paper and extracted this week's crossword which he laid out on top of the previously completed one. That done, a glass of wine, a little TV and it was off to bed.

During the next few mornings he tackled, as usual, the new crossword. This one seemed harder and it took him towards the end of the week to complete about three quarters of it. It was as he was scanning the thing to find a potentially easy group of clues when he noticed another line 'across' in which the words could be linked.

This was:-

SECRET # MEETINGS # OBSERVED

Richard was startled. Was this a deliberate association of words? If so, was this group linked to the previous one he had noticed?

Rational considerations prevailed and he tried to ignore the issue. But he did cut out the completed two crosswords, dated them, and set them aside in his miscellaneous file. But this did not prevent him from carefully scanning the next puzzle, which however as far as he could tell had none of the words which might be linked in some manner. And it became routine for him to check for linked words on completion of each crossword.

Thus it was several weeks later, and he had almost forgotten to check the latest, when a block of words stood out un-missably, and occupying two adjacent lines, it read:-

MARRIAGE # WRECKER
WILLBE # DESTROYED

This time the thing took a firm root in Richard's mind. He pondered the situation, the rest of the crossword forgotten. It could after all just be coincidence, or even a jest. He was inclined to dismiss it as irrelevant, but what if it was not? This prompted other questions. If it was a message - who was it intended for? How would the compiler, if it was he, know that it would be read by the person for whom it was intended, how could this be guaranteed? It seemed he had a puzzle within a puzzle.

***

Then he began to wonder about himself. Were the messages, that is if they were messages, intended for him? But he took a cool look at the likelyhood of this and dismissed it ---- for the moment.

However it did prompt him to examine his recent liaison. He had met Julie Chambers when on his summer holiday in Scotland. The end of a wet and dismal day had found him drowning his disappointment in a rather bare and unwelcoming hotel bar. His meal had just arrived, when in strode Julie.

Now there's a fine figure of a woman, he thought, a view that was reinforced as she abandoned her outdoor gear. There were only two other people present, two Scotsmen were imbibing whiskey chasers at the bar. They took little notice of the new visitor being deep in some argument of their own.

She smiled at him, and he felt a definite stirring in the region of his heart, something he had not felt for some time. Sadly, he thought, the evening ended as it had begun with him on his own.

The following day the weather was even worse and he gave walking a miss in favour of a lunchtime meal at the same hotel. Unattrective as it was he had to admit the food was excellent. And there she was. Already seated with a bottle of wine on her table, she waved a hand at him as he entered. He looked round for a place but this time the bar was crowded and there were no empty tables. As he was trying to decide what to do, the girl waved him over. `Hallo again,' she said. Her voice was warm and well modulated, she was also unmistakably English.

`Please do join me, I can't drink all this on my own.' She waved a vague hand towards the nearly full bottle.

`Are you sure?' He queried.

`If I wasn't, I wouldn't have asked,' she said mellowing the comment with a gorgeous smile that seemed to him to light up the whole room.

He sat.

It was the start of an intense relationship.

They had tons in common. They were both there on their own on walking holidays, both fed up with the almost continuous bad weather. Then oddly they found out that they were staying at the same hotel just down the road, and he wondered how he had missed her. They exchanged walking stories, and he discovered that she had been on most of the local mountains on previous trips and was now exploring the dramatic nearby coast with its wild and empty beaches and towering cliffs.

`I am desparate to see at least one wild otter, but so far I have had no luck.'

`Yes,' he agreed, `one does need a considerable amount of luck, I have seen them more than once. At one time feeding in and out of the kelp, and once I even saw a mother playing wih a pair of cubs in the loch.'

She was excited by this. `You lucky chap, do you think that if you took me we might see one. Oh do please let's try?'

Taken aback, and quite out of his depth, `OK,' he replied and began to drown.

She clapped her hands, and topped up his glass.

`Chances are we may not see anything,' he warned.

But it was too late.

They did not see an otter the next day, inspite of walking some distance along the coast, but they did see a pile of fish bones on a rocky ledge just above high water mark, which he thought was a regular otter feeding place. But by now otters were of secondary importance. They enjoyed each other's company and before retiring to their respective rooms Julie gave him a swift kiss by way of a thank-you.

Next day they watched the feeding spot and were delighted to see a male otter land and devour a mackrel almost as big as himself.

Julie was extatic and that night they shared his room.

Since then they had met fairly frequently, about once a month, and so far at a different hotel each time, apart from those occasions when she came to his home.

But now he began to wonder, just what did he know about her. After all he had from the start told her all about himself.

He found he did not know a single basic thing about her. He conducted a mental review -

Was she married? She had somehow implied that she had once been, and she did have rings on her wedding finger. He did not know.

Where did she live? She had never let slip, his only means of contact with her was by her mobile phone. She was adamant about this. Another un-known.

Had she a job? She let him think she had a well paid job, but what? Yet another blank.

Had she family?

Richard was stunned. After a close relationship of many months he still knew absolutely nothing about Julie. She was a person with no background and no history - she was in fact a puzzle.

Which brought him back to his crossword.

What if she was married and her husband, a crossword compiler, had discovered their relationship? After all she knew that he did this particular puzzle on a regular basis - could she have told her husband? Were the words intended for him?

That day Richard retired to bed a worried man.

But these concerns vanished in the cold light of dawn. He laughed at his paranoia of the previous evening as he spread the news sheet with the latest crossword out and prepared to enjoy a leisurely breakfast.

His confidence was short lived.

As he filled in the answers he felt a cold hand grip his heart.

One by one the words stood out.

```
                          A
            D             C
            R             T
            A             I
   # WIFES # LIAISON # GOESON
            T             N
            I
            C
```

This time he just knew it was meant for him. He would discus the situation with Julie when next they met.

But Richard was in for another shock.

A while later and in a calmer frame of mind he dialled Julies mobile phone number to arrange a meeting. He was stunned when one of those mechanical voices told him that `the number he had dialled was no longer available.'

He must have mis-dialled, so he tried again and third time, with exactly the same result.

It came horribly home to him then that he had absolutely no means of contacting Julie, and if his fears about the crossword were correct he could not warn her.

He could only hope that she might contact him, but after several sleepless nights and worrying days he knew that she wouldn't or couldn't, and decided on the only action he could think of. He contacted the newspaper. After several mis-transfers he was eventually connected to the man who claimed to set the puzzle. Not wishing to be thought a mental case and have the phone put down on him, he arranged a meeting for the following day.

Clasping his small file of the relevant crosswords Richard was conducted to a big room with two rows of desks each with its terminal and its operator. He was introduced to a bright looking middle aged Dan Broadbent who was responsible amongst other things for setting the crossword puzzles.

`Can we go somewhere more private?' Richard asked.

`Sure, we can use one of the interview rooms,' Dan said, `just follow me.'

`Well what's all this about?' Dan asked when they were seated in fairly comfortable chairs on each side of a large desk, on which was the inevitable computer screen and a telephone. He was hoping there might be a story in it.

Richard placed his folder on the desk and withdrew the crosswords, and somewhat diffidently Richard told Dan his story.

Dan's reaction was a surprise.

Instead of dismissing Richard's tale out of hand, he laid the puzzles out on the table in their correct chronological sequence and stared at them for some time in silence. Then he seemed to make up his mind. `Don't go away,' he said, `I want to bring in another of our staff.' And with this he left the room.

He was gone about five, to Richard, very long minutes.

`This is John Smeeton,' Dan said on his return, introducing a tall, lean chap with a concerned face. `He is our chief crime reporter,' and he introduced Richard. Dan sat whilst John Smeeton leaned over the desk to inspect the crosswords.

Richard was again taken by surprise, what the hell was going on?

John spoke, `You had better come clean,' he said to Dan.

`OK, but it's a long story,' Dan began. `The puzzles you have here are not new ones. They were originally compiled and published about three years ago. But we lost our proper crossword man and decided to repeat these old ones whilst we tried to find another compiler.

`The words you have highlighted were noticed the previous time they were published and someone brought them to the attention of the police. They found that the compiler's wife was missing, a fact he had neglected to report. His name was Alexander and although the police tried to trace his wife, she has never been found. However, it was discovered that she had been having an affair with a traveller in leather goods. He was as helpful as he could be but he had no idea where the lady was. She seemed to have vanished into thin air.'

Dan stopped and turned to the crime man, who took up the tale.

`Suspicion naturaly fell on the compiler, but nothing could be proved, in spite of the crossword evidence, it was decided that a jury would find the connection just too hard to believe. The police still keep the file open but we think to no avail.'

He paused, and smiled at the changes of expression on Richard's face as he began to grasp the fact that he was right about the crossword but relieved that it was not intended for him.

`So, what happened to Alexander?' He asked.

`Unfortunately for justice but possibly fortunately for him, he died peacefully of natural causes just about three weeks ago.'

***

Back home Richard found a message from Julie on his answering machine apologising for not contacting him for some time but without any explanation. She then stated her new mobile phone number.

But Richard was unsure if he wanted to reply, he would want answers to too many questions.

JML
20/1/2009

A VISIT FROM GOD

One day around what some humans know as two thousand and something AD, God woke up and found that he was bored. For a start there was no-one good enough to talk to. So he made contact with the Devil via one of his rather dubious angels, and suggested a chat for old times sake. The Devil, also not too busy, and fancying a change of company proposed they meet at some neutral ground half way between his place and God's. They chose the Earth.

It was early closing day in the small suburb on the outskirts of Manchester where they met, and they went un-noticed as they sat on the bench in the park. The odd passer-by simply took them to be foreigners - there were plenty of oddly garbed strangers around these days.

After exchanging notes on the various aches and pains they were suffering, and remedial suggestions, The Devil began musing aloud. 'You know,' he said, ' When were we last here? It was a hell of a long time ago, if you'll pardon the pun. But you are up there in your ivory tower and I'm down there in my lonely den and we have no idea what people get up to these days.'

'But I still have to do my judging,' protested God.

'No you damned well don't,' retorted The Devil, ' if you'll pardon the pun, things have got so busy that you delegate the job, just like I do. Look, it's only right that having written and agreed the Rule Book we can leave the hard work to others. It makes for an easy, er......time.'

'You're right, of course,' said God, 'but why should we bother?'

'Well for one thing, I keep getting told that things have changed and the Rule Book is out of date. Some have argued that deeds which once would have sent someone down to me are now considered acceptable, even legal. We may be doing some people a grave injustice, if you will pardon the pun. And eternity is quite a long time.'

God sat and thought.

'By heaven!' He said, 'if you'll pardon the pun. I think you may be right.'

Just then a rather attractive woman strode past with a small dog on a lead.

'Now that's what I call tasty,' said God.

'Just a moment old prune, you're God and not supposed to have any such thoughts,' protested his companion. 'That's my job, and I would send you for a spell in purgatory for that one alone if I had your job.'

'Just wait a cotton-pickin minute,' retorted God, 'you forget yourself. Now you are showing signs of godlike thoughts.'

And for some time they sat and mulled over this curious turn of events. Things had gone mad. Was it they both wondered because they were here on this little known planet? Whatever the reason they both felt they would like a change.

God spoke first.

'Do you know,' he began, 'I like this place and would very much like to stay here for a while.'

'God love us,' said The Devil, ' if you'll pardon the pun, so do I, why don't we ask the Boss? The others can manage perfectly well with our Rule Book.'

A proposal to which God happily agreed.

They had to apply for an audience with The Firmament, as Boss HE was eternally busy. There was always some new particle to invent to keep the scientists occupied and thus out of trouble. After all it had been a near thing with the atomic bomb.

Eventually they found themselves being escorted into HIS grand presence, where hesitantly they made their case.

'OK,' rumbled The Firmament, 'but be aware your jobs may not be available when you decide to return. Now if that's all I'm busy.'

'Hell's teeth,' said the Devil, 'if you'll pardon the pun, HE agreed.'

'Yes, so I'll see you in about an Earth year, if you think that should be enough?' God suggested.

'Fair enough,' agreed the Devil, 'be good!' And was gone.

***

Down on old Earth God soon found lots of things to his liking. He took to gambling especially at cards, and found that he was good at it, although being able to see what was in everyone's hand did help. He enjoyed a drink, and good food. The Earth gave him joy with its wonderful scenery, which he had to remind himself he had created, and all the amazing animals. Interestingly whilst he remembered starting the whole thing off, it had since evolved extensively and bore little resemblance to his original design - and he was rather pleased with how it had turned out.

But it was the females that he liked best, and very quickly learned some quite wicked but immensely thrilling things to do with them. All in all God was having a jolly good time.

Eventually, as with most things when carried to an excess, God got bored and decided to call it a day, albeit a very long day.

He applied to The Firmament.

`What you here again, you've only just left,' growled The Firmament, `what do you want now?'

`I would like to go back to my old job.' Said God.

`Sorry old boy but that position is taken. Your friend the Devil so enjoyed doing good things on Earth whilst he was there that he applied for you job, and since it was vacant I gave it to him. And a credit to it he has been.'

`Damnation!' Exclaimed God. `If you'll pardon the pun, but what's to become of me?'

`Well the Devil's old job is still open, you could do worse.'

God wondered just what worse was, and quickly made up his mind.

`I'll take it,' he said.

***

Eons later The Firmament took a check up of the Earth and was considerably surprised by the changes he saw. With God taking the Devil's job he had allowed a few naughty but pleasant activities, but being God had heavily condemned all really bad works and eventually had succeeded prevented them altogether.

Even more surprising was that the Devil had taken God's job to heart and was generating good deeds all over the place, and he was enjoying doing so. Kindliness and forgiveness were the watchwords on this new Earth. For the very first time in the history of that planet there was peace among men.

'Ah well!' Mused The Firmament, 'That's life,' if you'll pardon the pun.

JML
26/8/2008